THE CLEWER INITIATIVE

T. T. Carter and
The Fight Against Modern Slavery

THE CLEWER INITIATIVE

T. T. Carter and
The Fight Against Modern Slavery

Alastair Redfern

2017

The Clewer Initiative: T. T. Carter and The Fight Against Modern Slavery - Published by the Rev. Dr. Ashish Amos of the Indian Society for Promoting Christian Knowledge (ISPCK), Post Box 1585, Kashmere Gate, Delhi-110006.

ISBN: 978-81-8465-634-3

Laser typeset by

ISPCK, Post Box 1585, 1654, Madarsa Road, Kashmere Gate, Delhi-110006 • *Tel:* 23866323

e-mail: ashish@ispck.org.in • ella@ispck.org.in
website: www.ispck.org.in

Printed at Saurabh Printers, NOIDA.

For

Jane Olive CSJB

Mary Stephen CSJB

Anne CSJB

Elizabeth Jane CSJB

Monica CSJB

Ann Verena CJGS

Contents

Dedication ... *v*

Preface ... *ix*

Introduction ... *xi*

1. The Business of Slavery ... 1

2. A New Witness to Freedom ... 11

3. The Calling of Clewer ... 24

4. A House of Mercy ... 40

5. The Pursuit of Partnership ... 54

6. Hospitality ... 64

7. Confronting Sin and Owning Evil ... 77

8. Deep Cleansing for All ... 87

9. Clothed in Promises ... 98

10. Caught Up in the Cloud of Prayer ... 108

11. A Model of Catholic Mission ... 117

12. The Clewer Initiative Today ... 131

Preface

I have had the challenging privilege of becoming involved in the efforts in our society to fight against the evils of Modern Slavery. There are a number of key areas for engagement; legislation, policing, the identification, rescue and support of victims, better business practice, a moral indifference, the weakening of social cohesion and any sense of neighbourliness, the increasing desperation of refugees and vulnerable people.

As I have worked with churches, statutory and voluntary groups, politicians, business leaders, the media, faith communities, universities, schools and many other sectors, there has been a particular opportunity in the Diocese of Derby to build partnerships for making an effective response.

Several years ago representatives of the few remaining Sisters of the Community of St John Baptist, Clewer - now resident at Ripon College, Cuddesdon - approached me about the possibility of supporting the development and expansion of this work, through the network of Anglican Dioceses across England, but always in partnership with others.

The result has been the establishment of 'The Clewer Initiative'. A fitting legacy for the present generation of the Sisters of the

Community of St John Baptist, and a timely intervention through which our churches can be better equipped to play as full a part as possible in this battle against forces of evil which bring into sharp focus the challenges being faced through the processes of globalisation.

I hope that a reminder about the founding of the original Clewer Initiative might highlight wisdom and resources to inform and encourage our twenty-first century attempt to follow in these steps, and to craft a contribution equally valuable in our own times.

ℰ ℰ ℰ

Introduction

This book is an attempt to tell two stories. First, the development of a response to the challenges of Modern Slavery. Second, a reflection upon a similar initiative in nineteenth century England.

Both endeavours involve initiatives to identify and support victims, build effective partnerships and resources, and highlight issues to be addressed by individuals, by society, and by the Church.

The story of a creative response to the slavery of prostitution and alcohol abuse in Victorian society illustrates how a Christian concern for the vulnerable came to be expressed in an organised way through the foundation of a religious order of "Sisters of Mercy", based initially in a parish, and then expanding to other places of need in England and eventually overseas. This initiative emerged as a result of reflective leadership, personal calling and commitment, the support and blessing of the wider church, and the establishment of effective partnerships for every expression of the operation as it unfolded.

The issues identified and the actions pursued were testing points for the credibility of the Christian Gospel in an increasingly secular, urban, industrial and individualised world. This project offers a case study of creative reflection on the Gospel of Jesus Christ, faithful response for the wellbeing of others, and the development of new ways of witness and worship — all crafted to be appropriate to the challenges of a particular context.

II

A key strand of this story is the life of Thomas Thellusson Carter, and his own journey through Christian discipleship and leadership, first within a parochial setting, but then eventually by developing structures and strategies complementary to the parish system. His theological teaching is explored in some depth, so as to better appreciate his understanding of the call of God in a testing situation, and to help identify resources that can provide invaluable insights and models for our twenty-first century attempts to discern and respond to the call of the kingdom in a world where the phenomenon of Modern Slavery is a prime indicator of the reality of evil and the need for effective witness to the possibility and triumph of goodness and grace.

Alongside the theological insights and imperatives, the story of the Clewer Sisters and their host parish provides an example of how concern and commitment could be ordered for the service of the vulnerable and the proper inclusion of victims in the project of the coming of the Kingdom.

After a brief report about the pressing realities of Modern Slavery today, the journey of Carter and that of the Community of St John Baptist Clewer, is unfolded. The interplay of theological reflection and appropriate action illuminates the inspiring development of this story, and offers material to support more contemporary engagement.

The later chapters invite a deeper exploration of the values, practices and priorities for a Christian life called into this way of witness. These key elements are unfolded in relation to personal formation, and in terms of their implications for structures and the better ordering of the Christian contribution to the shaping of a society. The narrative highlights indications of the most appropriate and effective practices to best enable contemporary engagement. Further, there are pointers towards the wider implications for the future of the parish, as well as signs of how more focussed forms of Christian witness and social action might be offered. Some of these possibilities are highlighted in the final chapter, which attempts to draw conclusions from the teaching and theological wisdom of T.T. Carter. His approach to forming this effective Christian initiative gives many clues to crafting a catholic model of mission fully connected with the issues and values of the modern world.

The contemporary challenge is for the Clewer Initiative to prove itself worthy of this legacy.

1

The Business of Slavery

Slavery in History

Slavery is a very ancient institution. It was justified by Aristotle as a natural ingredient of society. Slaves were not fully human, but fulfilled a necessary and important function in the making of the social fabric. In both Greek and Roman culture slaves were a key part of the economy, and of the social structure - people totally at the call and service of others.

Slavery and the Gospel

It is significant that Jesus the Lord and Messiah chose a particular word to describe His role and ministry – doulos – or slave. Modern translations of the New Testament often soften the impact of this startling and unique choice of designation by using the more acceptable term 'servant'. In the late twentieth century as welfare became professionalised in the west, churches found a niche by offering a 'servant' ministry. An approach that tended to miss the point of this significant choice of terminology.

The First 'Abolition'

In 2007 there were worldwide celebrations of the two hundredth anniversary of the Abolition of the Slave Trade associated with William Wilberforce. At the same time, the phenomenon of 'modern' slavery was developing exponentially. The modern slave trade is second only to drugs as a lucrative criminal business, and continues to expand.

Modern Slavery

Modern Slavery includes forced labour, sex trafficking, domestic servitude, organ trafficking, highly organised begging, and forced marriage. It is widespread in almost every country and sheltered in many areas by cultural norms which endorse massively unequal social hierarchies and the subservience of women and children. This expanding and systematic abuse of human beings operates through smart businesses organised by criminal elements using sophisticated systems of organisation and accounting. There are a number of factors enabling and encouraging this expansion of the commodification of people.

Opportunities for Oppression

In terms of business culture, there tends to be a less close relationship between employer and employees. The mobility of the work force, and the pressure of tight margins and the need for flexibility has had the effect of employers using an increasing amount of labour provided by agencies. This gives space for unscrupulous operators to import or recruit people whose passports are confiscated, often they are told that they owe a huge sum for transportation, and the traffickers also know the whereabouts of people's families and their situation. Further, the 'business model' works because traffickers are very skilled at recruiting vulnerable people who can be easily manipulated and controlled. These groups of workers can be crowded into poor accommodation and bussed to and from work, salaries paid into bank accounts controlled by the traffickers, with one of the controllers always acting as interpreter and negotiator. Sometimes benefits are also claimed on behalf of those enslaved in this way.

A similar model would be girls and women (sometimes males) attracted to a new place by the promise of what looks like regular 'work' - only to be put into brothels, with huge 'debts' to pay off. The pain of being raped repeatedly each day sometimes leads to drug dependency. The same process can be experienced by people seeking domestic work.

In all cases victims are told not to trust the police, who will only punish them further. This increases a sense of isolation, dependency and helplessness. There seems to be no space for hope or seeking help.

The Search for a New Social Contract

This trade in people is fuelled by the increasing volume of those displaced by war or violence, or simply seeking a taste of what they perceive to be a 'better' life – easily glimpsed via the internet and mobile phones. Whatever strategies are employed as short term responses to this huge mobility of 'vulnerable' people – the longer term fact is that such mobility and pressure to push back against this increasingly transparent inequality is going to be a much more normal factor within the dynamics of world citizenship. More enduring solutions will need to be crafted. Those who recognise the reality of this challenge to global stability will need to help to craft a new kind of contract – creating a richer degree of connectivity and mutuality than has been recognised by the post Reformation development of nation states and more recent forms of the narrowing identities of tribalism and face-book type groupings.

Measure for our Future

The battle against Modern Slavery will be a litmus test of what such richer connectivity and mutuality might be able to look like – both at the macro level in terms of Government policies and international co-operation, and also through the more local partnerships between voluntary, statutory and specialist agencies to identify, support and rehabilitate 'victims'. The treatment of those abused by the commodification of human beings will be a key indicator of our potential to craft more just and more inclusive ways of relating within the powerful forces of a market driven international economy alongside a radical claiming of freedoms for movement and development by individuals, including the poorest and those displaced by the inevitabilities of tensions and conflicts.

The Globalisation of Indifference

Besides the 'business' model and pressure for low costs meeting the desperation of vulnerable people willing to face huge risks in an unknown future, Modern Slavery also thrives because of a general cultural phenomenon which Pope Francis has called "The Globalisation of Indifference".

This phenomenon thrives because of the sheer busy-ness of people in their personal lives - illustrated by the huge focus upon a very small screen (mobile phone) through which life is lived. Such is the narrowness of this personal focus, paradoxically while accessing the world in terms of news, information and a whole host of website type opportunities for communication, that we never 'look up' to notice what is happening around us. Modern Slavery thrives because in our busyness to organise and enjoy our 'personal' life, we do not really pay attention to factors such as the low cost of some clothing, the fact that many phones contain cobalt which is produced largely through child labour, or the amazingly cheap availability of services such as nail bars or car washes.

Increasingly people are so busy paying attention to their own immediate agendas that they fail to notice what is happening to others – through the systems, products and processes that provide the infrastructure and services for modern life. This is a form of 'indifference' that creates space for a growing black market in terms of business practice, and the brutal exploitation of fellow human beings to provide labour, sexual and domestic services, or even organs on market rather than medical principles.

The second major cause of the globalisation of indifference is the over-development of modern liberalism. Since the Reformation and the Enlightenment there has been an important, precious and amazing movement towards individual freedom and the associated structures to generate 'toleration' of the magnification of differences that such a process has inevitably produced. This explosion of differences of identity and aspiration can be seen in areas such as gender, sexuality, politics, moral values and market placements.

The End of Liberalism

Besides the inevitable increase in tensions and conflict, so evident in political and religious spheres especially, there has been a growth in the idea of 'toleration' that has shifted beyond giving space to the differences in others, to simply ignoring those who are different. This can feel like a grown-up, fully developed 'liberalism': "I in my small corner, you in yours" – giving the 'other' total space and freedom to be 'different', except when this comes back to bite us in activities such as terrorist attacks. Such advanced toleration in fact becomes a violent form of indifference – with no real interest in the values of others, except when outcomes trespass upon 'my' own preferences. The result is the creation of space for enormous abuse of the vulnerable and needy by unscrupulous manipulators. This is most graphically illustrated by the huge explosion of pornography, the growth of a 'sex industry' and the resulting enslavement of millions of people.

A tragic example would be the story of a British girl who left home as a young teenager and was drawn into sex slavery, first in a brothel in London, and then for six years in a brothel in the Middle East. She was trapped by being in a foreign culture, with no language skills, no passport and the threat of brutal violence is she failed to co-operate.

For all of this time she longed for someone to ask 'how are you?' No-one did. She was expected to play her part in the adult liberal world in which each person can do as they choose with whom, when they want to. A presupposition that financial transaction undergirded universal participation in the 'adult' free world. Each participant was playing their part but there was no space or interest in the other as a 'person' needing to relate in a broader and more complex way. The entire emphasis was upon pursuing 'answers' to the immediate desires of those with the means to purchase their satisfaction, rather than asking questions about hopes, potential and the fulfilling of a person in a sustainable, grace-giving, mutual way. This 'liberal' world was too busy and too focussed on the assumption of each person looking out for themselves within their own sphere of 'choice' and 'possibility', so that there was no space for risking the questions that open up a deeper agenda. No-one asked this victim 'how are you?' There was no recognition of a connectivity that might point to mutuality, let alone any notion of putting the weakest first.

Such practices are 'tolerated' by a mis-shapen liberalism. It can often seem as though the only form of putting a 'boundary' upon such toleration is around the notion of 'children'. Our care for children still seems to be able to generate paying attention to those outside of our own lifestyle, and to recognising the point of joined-up public concern.   However the irony is that even this residual boundarying of toleration is not adequate to stop a terrifying rise in the abuse and exploitation of children, especially for the satisfaction of adult sexual desires, and for the provision of the cheapest of cheap labour.   By way of example the illustrated book by Lisa Kristine (Bound To Freedom) powerfully displays the sheer horror of forced labour in brick factories in India[1].

Redefining Freedom

Once again, there is an urgent need for new forms of connectivity and mutuality to be crafted and exemplified – particularly to involve those most abused and excluded by the indifference of contemporary toleration.   There is an important opportunity for a revised understanding of freedom – as a quality in human life that can only be realised within the context of our cohabitation with others. There is a challenge to rediscover some of the values that crafted modern institutions and values such as the nation, the corporation, the nuclear family, the interconnectivity of the market and the 'social' context of every human life.

Such a movement will need to converge around the fact that for any individual to be 'free', this will require the security and stability of 'community' as a prior reality and value.   Similarly we need to re-establish the moral role of the state, as guardian not just of the least restrictions on individual liberty imaginable, but as shaper and promotor of mutual flourishing as the essential context for individual development.   There is a reality of common life from which no-one can opt out, if 'society' is to be healthy and sustainable through all these pressures of development, difference and defensiveness.

Partnerships

At local and more intermediate levels we will need to recapture the energy and effectiveness of partnerships - in political and civic spaces. Partnerships for particular purposes, and mechanisms to connect and nourish partnerships, crucial elements in the greater enterprise of human community. There is a universal reality which makes every 'experience' relative and needing to own a greater connection. This is the task of political and social reshaping that those involved in the battle against Modern Slavery can contribute towards – by the values and models of good practice around the inclusion and rehabilitation of 'victims', and in terms of challenging corrupt and dehumanising practices, not least though developing models of effective partnership and community cohesion based upon recognition of the importance of some kind of 'common good'.

The driver will not be the creation of finalised 'systems' – but the identification and pursuit of 'potential'. In Mexico girls and women rescued from brothels are offered 'care' which eventually includes the opportunity to be given a blank sheet of white paper, on which to write or draw their aspirations. For someone abused, bullied and oppressed, this is a space that for so long has seemed closed and impossible. A further stage involves not just the seeking of education, training or other opportunities to pursue this personal potential, but also to learn how an individual vocation can only grow and mature in relation to others. Modern Slavery is about the commodification of human bodies. St Paul recognised that each human body is a temple of the Holy Spirit. That is, a clean sheet upon which God can draw and nourish aspirations, as part of a wholeness or Holiness that enables each person to be part of a greater 'Body': the Body of Christ – made up of many members, some apparently unseemly, and yet each with a vital though uniquely different part to play. Personal potential grows through participation in partnership – the connectivities that create 'community'.

New Life

In this sense the recognition of, and response to, Modern Slavery requires us to design new structures and institutions to handle this invitation to identify potential and find ways of pursuing it in a 'holy' and wholesome way. Any notion of 'rights' can only be pursued within this context of mutual responsibilities for the wellbeing of the 'whole' (Holy) through which the parts can best flourish and become themselves.

This reality in the human condition provides a key context for the need to challenge the globalisation of indifference. The design of systems needs to be supported and supplemented by signs, ritual, representation of possibilities and values. The partnership approach to be explored in the following chapters will give indications of what this ecology might look like, and what kind of perspectives and rationales might contribute not just to the wellbeing of victims and the campaign against slavery, but also provide models and ways of paying attention to the inevitable 'otherness' of human life that could highlight valuable contributions to the more general wellbeing of society.

In terms of Christian faith the call is to honour incarnation - the Enfleshment of God's life through the creation of human beings, highlighted in Jesus Christ. Further, to embrace and accept atonement: the cleansing reorientation from self to God and neighbour – the way of the cross, a way of inevitable struggle, misunderstanding and set back. And finally to receive resurrection, a new life, a new spirit of wholeness through which perfection of our potential as creatures can be given grace and taken more fully into God's final purposes in the glory of eternity. Each of these dynamics provides points of challenge and nourishment - not in a simple linear way of unending progress through perfection, but as a deepening engagement with this rich reality of challenges and possibilities.

The story of Clewer as a particular initiative emerges out of the global reality of the ever increasing growth of Modern Slavery, the efforts of particular people to recognise and challenge such a vicious and live-destroying phenomenon, and reflections about the purpose and potential that can be identified by examining such a call and its possible consequences for human wellbeing.

Endnotes

[1] Lisa Kristine, Bound To Freedom, Goff Books 2017.

2

A New Witness to Freedom

A Political Context

A Christian response to the rise of Modern Slavery will be part of our daily prayer for the coming of the kingdom. Jesus chose this provocative political image to encapsulate His teaching and His message. A kingdom is a single, all embracing working unit within which each person is a citizen who has to find their place. All under a Sovereign Head who holds a common sense of purpose and the power of pursuing ways of its unfolding. A king and a kingdom provide a purpose, a power, and a frame within which citizens are unavoidably connected. This context is the only one that can provide proper fulfilment and freedom.

Inclusivity

Those enslaved or denied 'citizenship' are less than full participants. The choice of the notion of kingdom is the sharpest reminder of the radical and total inclusivity we see in the Gospel of Jesus Christ. Positive engagement with rich and poor, sinners and righteous religious people, the 'chosen' people and those beyond, both the sick and the healthy. New life in the kingdom is an all embracing invitation with the most radical social and political consequences.

The current challenge of Modern Slavery is a key litmus test of the viability of this Gospel in the modern world. A moment to demonstrate how mercy can meet markets around the terrible fact of the commodification of human beings.

St Paul imitates this radically inclusive 'catholicity' with his foundational image of the Body. One Head, a multiplicity of parts, each with a particular role and contribution, joined in a common life.

Compassion Calling

Much gospel witness involves noticing and paying attention to those excluded by the narrowing tendencies of human selfishness. And one of the amazing outcomes of such a focussing of our energies and aspirations is the fact that in human hearts there is a deep instinct of compassion. A desire to suffer with, and to support those in need, and an aspiration to raise them up into a more supportive and inclusive place. Jesus appeals to this 'spirit' in the Sermon on the Mount. The Beatitudes invite each of us to own our deep instinct for peace, justice, purity and rescue from oppression, including enslavement to riches and personal agendas.

We see this reality of the human condition when there is a 'disaster' reported in the media – followed by an outpouring of concern, identification, prayer and practical responses. These moments of the connectivities created by compassion indicate the possibility for a fuller human flourishing and the potential of each of us to play a contributing part.

Those who join in the fight against Modern Slavery experience this deep sense of compassion, common cause and connected futures. The horror and scale of the challenge surfaces a 'spiritual' response – a common spirit seeking 'wholeness' – a meeting of hearts knowing that goodness and grace can be possible. There emerges a spiritual cohesion that transcends and knits together differences of faith, political persuasion or personal lifestyle.

The process of working together, engaging with victims and perpetrators, and forming partnerships in such a cause, shifts cohesion to a spiritual passion which becomes committed to paying attention to 'others', reflecting and asking appropriate questions of dubious or damaging practices, and discerning responses to enable better health for individuals and for society.

A Personal Calling

To explore these processes and their potential I propose to examine an early prototype in the modern world – the formation and leadership of a religious community in Clewer, near Windsor, in the nineteenth century. This will provide wisdom about practices and perspectives that might be helpful to a continuing Christian response and contribution.

The key thread will be the journey of a person, Thomas Thellusson Carter, and his work in this particular parish. It is a story of a growing wisdom, the provision of practical structures, and an amazing effect into the wider world, reaching India and America among other places.

Since each of us is called and challenged to recognise the fact of our citizenship and the consequent opportunities and responsibilities, the narrative will begin with Carter's personal journey – his sense of call and its continuing refinement. He was to learn that the call of the King was to shift from the relative security and stability of being part of a church, a community, a family, a workplace – to recognising that all of these necessary contexts need to be recognised primarily as a particular expression of what he came to call a 'House of Mercy'.

Thomas Thellusson Carter was born in 1808. This moment, when the eighteenth century age of 'enlightenment' was moving into the nineteenth century as a time of industrialisation and the expansion of 'democracy', was not unlike the context which we face in the twenty-first century. During his lifetime there was an enormous expansion of technical competence, organisational structures, and aspirations for human flourishing. By the end of the nineteenth century there was an increasingly loud rhetoric about socialism, communism and the importance of including people. The simplest barometer would be the steady extension of the 'right' to vote, culminating in votes for women in 1918. Much like the increasing rhetoric about the importance of human rights in our modern world. However, the irony which Carter experienced, and which we need to notice, is that there is an almost direct correlation between the volume of this rhetoric of rights and inclusion, and the sheer fact of increasing inequality, exclusion ad extreme poverty. This unacknowledged but very potent dynamic was to produce a real spiritual crisis – and enormous political and social tensions. A similar process of disillusionment is proving to be a strong force in the first decades of the twenty-first century.

His father was Vice-Provost at Eton College near Windsor; and because he was a staff member, the boy was allowed to live at home in a family and community. This was a real blessing as public schools at the time could be very brutal places, with bear baiting, cock fighting and in Carter's time a violent culture of fights on the playing field - and in at least one of them a pupil was killed by another pupil. Public schools could be very violent communities with little control and limited learning. Carter saw what human beings could become – in the absence of appropriate structures and formation. But Carter was privileged to live in a family where there was a totally different sense of community.

A Separated Religion

It was the same in terms of his religious formation. The boys at school had one moment of formal religion every week - on a Sunday afternoon. The whole school was assembled and someone read what was described as an "inaudible prayer" and then there was a portion of "Blair's sermons". Readings from the works of a stolid, didactic eighteenth century preacher, mentioned by Jane Austen in Mansfield Park and Northanger Abbey. Religion was highly formalised: the reading of a prayer and then of a sermon – it was purely formal and conformity was sufficient. This remains a continuing danger for any religious practice and its institutionalisation for more widespread consumption. There is a constant temptation for religion to become formal, uncritical and unconnected with the rest of life. Carter realised that this kind of religion was marginal to people's lives and had become a matter of simple conformity. It did not seem to make any difference in the real world and that is what challenged him as he grew up.

He left Eton and went to study at Oxford University – at a college called Christ Church. Aedes Christi – the house of Christ – a faint echo of how, for him, the house of Christ could only be described as a house of mercy.

Two things that are significant from his account of this time at university. First of all the bed was too short, and secondly he had a very hot fireplace and very cold windows. He wrote home that he lived in the climate of the West Indies and of Siberia, and he moved constantly from one to the other. He offers this reflection to his parents because it made him think that the world somehow is not simply made to fit us. Consequently we are tempted to spend a significant amount of time trying to fit the world around what would suit us – in his case, make a longer bed, or turn the heating down and block up the windows. The quest he was to explore in his ministry was to what extent are we called to make the world fit ourselves better? or to what extent do we put up with some things so that we can help the world fit other people better? That is the big challenge to the human situation which Carter was beginning to discern. From being a baby at the breast we cry, we are fed, and the world is organised around our needs. As a very young man he became concerned about the tendency to become too focussed upon making the world fit around himself, because there were other people who the world did not seem to fit at all.

Faith in First Steps

This was the time of the first stirrings of the Oxford Movement, the recovery of a focus upon the church, the sacraments and the sacred ministry. Newman was preaching at St Mary's in Oxford. But this was not seen as a new spiritual opportunity by the established forces of religion. At his college chapel attendance was compulsory and the services were timed to prevent the students from going to Newman's service across the road. There can be a defensiveness about religion – encased in formality and uncritical repetition. What Carter learned at Oxford most clearly is that, in an age of enlightened reason where everything can be logical and worked out, little space was available for an imaginative pursuit of the big questions such as "is there a God?" "What happens after death?" "Why do people suffer?" There were no clear answers to these eternal issues. What Newman and others taught is that reason can take us to what was termed 'a balance of probabilities'. So that, for instance, our world is such a wonderful complex thing that it almost certainly must have been created with a purpose. Similarly, if we are all so amazingly different yet in the same environment there must be some force or power that connects us. On these large issues, reasoning could point to a balance of probabilities but Newman proposed that there is something in human hearts that takes a step which we call 'faith' (and which he termed the illative sense). This faculty moves us from thinking that it is quite likely that there is a God, to knowing more deeply that we can assent to this as reality. A similar faith can arise in the face of challenge or suffering, and nonetheless fill us with a confidence and a hope that goodness and grace will somehow triumph. A movement of the heart, which is a deeper register than the most precise calculations of the mind. In a later sermon Carter said "Reason leads us to the threshold of the sanctuary, faith enters within it."[1]

In human souls there is a deep faith which surfaces in times of testing, as with our earlier example of huge disasters. A deep connecting 'compassion' is never far below the surface and this is the seed of what becomes faith. This kind of faith cannot easily be written down, or captured in a formula to convince somebody else. Yet, there is something in human beings that senses and can believe and trust in goodness and grace, even against the odds – something beyond reasoning or simple written expression. This emphasis upon sacraments as signs of this faith-producing and nourishing process, and the exploring of the mystery of the human instinct for goodness, became the germ of his spirituality. A spirituality that whatever the evidence seems to indicate, we will try and do better for the sake of our fellow human beings who are suffering, because we feel a connection and an active compassion to call us to respond by owning a communion or spiritual commonness, and a call to pursue our shared potential for richer possibilities.

Enlarging the Perspective
When Carter finished university, he and a group of friends went exploring in Europe. They knew that there was a bigger world and

they wanted to see a larger perspective. He recognised that in order to fulfil his vocation he had to step away from his own comfortable space and learn to see from a different angle. This is what going to Europe was for many of young people at that time. For a Christian vocation the call is to learn to see oneself in God's world, always from a wider angle, particularly the perspectives of other cultures, values and practices.

He was ordained in 1832 and he went to be a curate in Reading. The first thing that happened when he arrived was that the vicar went away for six weeks and he was suddenly on his own. The church had a clerk, who would wait by the church door to help welcome people and organise public worship, which happened on Sunday, Wednesday and Friday. The clerk would wait by the door and if nobody came, he would come down to the vestry and say 'no prayers today'. He presupposed a formal service industry – there would be no prayers unless people came. A formal religious transaction. Echoes of Eton Chapel.

Finding a Frame

During his curacy Carter met and married Mary Anne Gould, and they had a very happy marriage. His own experience of a marriage that was enriching for him and his wife provided an important resource and perspective for his subsequent work with sexual slavery and gender exploitation. The path of a personal calling is a significant factor in the reshaping and sensitivities of a public work and witness, and a key base from which to explore and operate.

Equal Rights Obscure Inequality

In 1838 he became a vicar of the parish of Piddlehinton near Weymouth and when the locals heard that he did not shoot or fish they wondered what on earth he would spend his time doing. The expectations of worship were very low, as were the expectations of the clergy! When he arrived he discovered a tradition that at Christmas the vicar gave everyone in the village a mince pie, a loaf of bread and a quart of ale. He recognised that most of the people in that parish did not need these resources, but the custom was that everybody received the same gift – equality: an echo of that great liberal ideal that everybody is the same and all have the same rights, which each chooses how to handle according to their own personal preferences and desires.

Of course this custom probably began as a way of a previous vicar wanting to signal his care for every family in the parish. However, there were some people who were very poor, marginalised and excluded. As he discovered this reality, Carter decided to spend the money not on giving everybody a mince pie, a loaf of bread and a quart of ale, rather he used the resources for creating a club for clothing, and a food collecting point: structures for more thorough care and sharing. There was uproar in the parish because everyone thought they were entitled to their mince pie, and wanted a religion that was uncritically comfortable and collusive with the status quo. The rhetoric of equal rights obscured the realities of inequality. It is only when we look more carefully and pay close attention, that we notice the fact that there are people who are missing out, people who are hurting, people who may have the rights but they do not have the means to be able to benefit from them. These are the people who are being oppressed and abused by the way society tries to operate; and for Carter someone had to accept the call to look out for the vulnerable, make a stand and offer them some kind of priority. Carter began his public ministry by making this stand for people who were on the edge and outside. Paying attention to the realities beneath the rhetoric of equality, forming a new, more inclusive perspective, and developing appropriate models of better practice. Establishing a project based upon a working partnership that was willing to be counter cultural, for the sake of the vulnerable and oppressed.

A Range of Responses

This personal journey and clarifying of a Christian calling can be illustrated from a sermon Carter preached in 1856 when he was involved in the founding of the House of Mercy in Clewer. The sermon explored the sheer complexity of owning our identity as a spiritual person called to participate in a kingdom context.[2]

The text is from St John, chapter 19; describing the scene where a small group stand at the foot of the cross. Jesus is on the cross, beneath stand Mary the mother of Jesus, John the faithful friend, Mary's sister, and Mary Magdalene, often characterised as the sinner from the city. Mary Magdalene was the one who knelt at the feet of Jesus and washed his feet with her tears. A picture of a true penitent.

The House of Mercy was to help those who in the nineteenth century were called penitents – people who had been in prostitution and sexual slavery and who were now seeking God's wholeness, forgiveness and new life. Mary Magdalene was an important figure to the project in Clewer as someone who had taken that step from slavery to salvation.

There is a sense that each of us, if we stop to reflect, could stand in any of those four places at the foot of the cross. Each of us like Mary the Mother of Jesus, has a connection with a family – the context of relationship and responsibility which gives us life. Similarly, like St John, each of us knows something about friendship. More, like the sister of Mary, each of us also knows people who are distant relatives – that is we live in a bigger circle of people who are more distant and yet somehow connected. Lastly, like

Mary Magdalene the penitent, each of us is a sinner who seeks to be forgiven and restored. Carter suggested that our spiritual life is explored by recognising that each of us is all four 'types' at the same time. The temptation of the spiritual life is to say 'I am Mary the Mother, part of the close family of Jesus': or, 'I am Jesus' special friend, like John: therefore especially privileged as a disciple'; or again 'I am more like a distant relative with a more nebulous connection'; or finally 'I am a hopeless sinner, totally dependent, with nothing to contribute'.

Too often we identify with one of these characters – but there can be a challenge to recognise a more complex call. If we are honest about our spiritual life, we inhabit this kind of range of possibilities. What we need to do is to recognise that each of those spiritual states lives in us. One might predominate at one time and one at another, but we must beware thinking that we can just be like Mary, John, Mary's sister, or Mary Magdalene. We will always be some kind of challenging mix, which is why spirituality rests upon the foundation of prayers of confession.

Recognising the complexity within our characters and their formation, as well as the potential tensions between ourselves and others, is important in seeking the most effective ways of negotiating partnerships with potential allies, as well as learning to read the textured nature of the institutions and individuals whom we try to challenge and call to change. This theme will be explored more fully in a subsequent chapter.

Double Standards – Gender

A major strand in this sermon was to highlight another complexity about identity – that is the appalling double standard with regard to men and women. In his time when prostitution was such an enormous problem he highlighted a culture which held that the man can sin, that is engage with prostitution, and then return to his normal life. If the woman sins she is an outcast and unacceptable in society. This is not dissimilar to our context today, in which many people in slavery, especially sexual slavery, are women and girls. There continues to be a double standard about gender. Providers are criminalised and judged by society, purchasers of sex are accepted as simply exercising their choices as consumers of pleasure from a range of desirable products.

If we look at those four figures highlighted in the sermon, we will see that John is a kind of spiritual superstar because he wrote a gospel which is poetic and mystical but the others barely have a word between them. Mary, Jesus' mother, has one or two sentences and her sister and Mary Magdalene say very little. One of the things Carter recognised as needing to be confronted is the culture which gives men an over-honoured place that obscures other contributions and puts women in a place where they are too easily overlooked, abused, marginalised and have less of an opportunity to be noticed as more than commodities, and thus to participate in society more fully.

Double Standards: Wealth and Poverty

Carter goes on to argue that this is not just a gender divide. Wealthy people can engage in prostitution and get away with it. It is the poor and especially girls, who are vulnerable and need money, often becoming disconnected from their families, and thus tending to become drawn into selling themselves, thereby contributing to the success of the business of slavery. There is a double standard not just between men and women but between rich and poor. One of challenges in making a response to slavery is to beware of reinforcing such differences. There have been some signs of progress towards greater gender equality such as the ordination of women in the Church of England, but if we look at society generally, there is ample evidence which indicates that the movements towards giving women a proper and equal place are strong on rhetoric yet with very few real steps forward.   Hard evidence, such as the number of women in senior posts or the levels of earnings of women in work indicate that there is still a serious double standard and disparity. As some sections of society become wealthier and the one percent own more and more, there are an increasing number of people who have very little at all.

In Carter's time the vulnerable who were so easily not noticed, were the women and girls who had been drawn into prostitution because they had little option in trying to look after themselves, or limited alternatives in terms of other support systems. Similarly vulnerable people today are being drawn into slavery because they have very few other options and they are desperate – with others willing to take advantage for the sake of financial gain, under the cloak of a free, tolerant society presupposing choices within a market environment.   Reality is expressed through commodification and purchasing power.

Endnotes
[1] T.T. Carter: Meditation: Sermons, Longmans 1875.
[2] T.T. Carter: Mercy For The Fallen. Masters 1856.

3

The Calling of Clewer

Carter was learning about the complex dynamics of a personal spiritual journey and its practical outcomes. His education and family formation led to the recognition of a call to ordination in the Church of England, and service as a curate, and then as an incumbent.

This unfolding of vocation highlighted the importance of a critical and creative engagement with the unfinished and often struggling world within which he had learned to offer a daily prayer for the coming of a greater kingdom. There was no neat progression, but always a challenge to discernment of a more inclusive perspective and practice.

In 1844 he became the Rector of Clewer which was near Windsor, a living in the gift of Eton College. Although he resigned from this role in 1880, he remained as Warden of the Community of St John Baptist until his death in 1901, and thus was resident for fifty-seven years. That is noteworthy because we tend to live in a world where there is an emphasis upon progression. Fifty-seven years is an interesting challenge to the fast world we inhabit, where measurement of effectiveness is so often based on movement.

Clewer was a very run down part of Windsor – a great slum area. At one time church life had been looked after by a curate, who lived in a hotel in Piccadilly and simply took the train on Sundays in order to take the services to support formal religious observance as a model of ministry. When Carter arrived he was somewhat alarmed, as vicars often are, by the people who seemed to constitute the church. As in many churches there was a font where people are baptised and drawn into the Body of Christ. The font in Clewer church was where people put their hats and coats when they arrived, it was like an open cloakroom. They also had a strange custom whereby the churchwardens collected the offerings of the people. In those days Holy Communion took place very infrequently. The churchwardens used half of the offerings collected at services to give to people as inducements to come to Holy Communion. There was a mercenary spirituality in the parish. It was in a perilous state as well as including an area of serious poverty.

Building the Body

How was he to help this place discover a kingdom vocation? The first thing he did – and this is important for us when there is a great temptation to start by earning trust and connection through service – a servant ministry - is that he built up the church to be self-consciously the Body of Christ in that place.[1] He organised what was called at that time 'cottage meetings' i.e. he went into people's homes. There were often two or three families living in just a couple of rooms but he and his curate visited and they tried to listen, to discover the particular 'need' of the kingdom agenda, in order to unfold the gospel into the lives of people in the locality. He did not tell them to come into church to be simply taught and formed, rather he went into people's homes and got to know them. He tried to make a witness by loving, and by being present in people's lives. He established a benefits society to enable people to pool their small resources so that when something unexpected happened, such as a funeral or an unforeseen expense, a sum could be withdrawn. An important foundation to enabling people to join in finding connection in need and supporting one another. Further, there was a plot of land near the vicarage and it was made available for allotments, in order to help people grow food, and again learn to make provision for themselves, alongside others. Vocation unfolding through exploring connectivity in a particular context. Those in most need were full participants in any schemes to improve their oppressed situation.

Living By Giving

Perhaps more surprisingly, he also encouraged people to give to the SPG – the Society for the Propagation of the Gospel. Although there was tremendous need, so that he began by engaging with this reality in the place where he was trying to nourish the Body of Christ, and the coming of the kingdom, yet, there was always other need further afield that should be recognised. He taught the poorest of the poor that there would always be other people who needed help in other parts of the world. Partnership was to enable communion between the poorest, a common expressing of the spiritual values of the Beatitudes.

Upstairs

The Bishop of Oxford at this time was Samuel Wilberforce, one of the children of William Wilberforce, who had led the great fight against the slave trade. Samuel Wilberforce became the Bishop of Oxford at the age of forty and he unfolded a lively and ground breaking ministry in the leadership of the Church of England. Wilberforce used to say "Mr Carter is often upstairs". He did not mean that Carter was doolally! What he meant was that Carter engaged with people and the real context, but always had a vision of what was further afield. There was a sense about him that his mind was always drawn into a prayerfulness – on earth as it is in heaven. To perceive our vocation on earth we need to seek the perspective of God's overview of us, and of the world: the inner life and its outward manifestations. This higher view more fully reveals what the kingdom should be.

Carter was a man who gave a great deal of time to prayer. He was always ready to pray with and for others. When the Bishop said "Mr Carter is often upstairs" it was a compliment. He wanted to see the place he inhibited, on earth, through the eyes of heaven and therefore he needed to be a person of prayer. And, in his experience, those who prayed most deeply for the new transforming life of the coming Kingdom were those in the clearest need. People with more secure situations tended to pray for stability and personal progression.

Then as now, sadly, women were the barometer of the depth and nature of poverty, of the lack of opportunity, and of how oppression was being expressed. In the parish of Clewer there were a significant number of 'fallen women', as the Victorians called them. Many of these women were prostitutes, drawn by their poverty and vulnerability into this destructive trade. Others were women who had just fallen out of the system of family and community, including 'servants' who had been seduced or raped while in service and then dismissed with no kind of reference. There was a great deal of disease and often families perished. If people were destitute and could not find a job, there was no welfare provision, and it was common for several families to share a small living space. Clewer was a very vulnerable society for many of its inhabitants. The most vulnerable were women, not least because women had no legal rights and could not own property. Women were totally dependent on having a husband, father or brother. If a woman did not have a male figure in her life she would be very vulnerable to the pressure of pimps and punters. Not least because of the double standards which Carter had quickly perceived in relation to gender.

Penitentiaries

As he began his ministry in Clewer, in the wider church there was a movement to form what contemporaries called 'penitentiaries'. It is a great Victorian word. Penitence provides an accent on the negative – seeing others as those who need to be penitent. The task of the church was to help the fallen to own their 'fallenness' and thus be able to seek forgiveness. Archdeacon Manning was Samuel Wilberforce's brother in law. He eventually became a Roman Catholic priest and then Cardinal Manning, Archbishop of Westminster. At this time he was Archdeacon of Chichester. He preached a widely reported sermon in 1844 about saints and penitents, showing that both were on the same continuum of falling short and needing salvation.[2]

Shortly afterwards an Anglican priest called John Armstrong, the Vicar of Chepstow, began to publish articles arguing that the women who had fallen out of the system were not just a social problem, but the sign of a spiritual challenge for a society that was not seeing with the eyes of heaven and thus simply discarding them like rubbish.[3] In 1852 the Church Penitentiary Association was formed to create structures and resources to deal with penitents.

There was an interesting manifestation of this wider movement from the pen of The Revd Samuel Fox, who was Rector of Morley in Derbyshire. In 1845 he published a book about monks and monasticism. Generally monasteries had been abolished during the Reformation, but Fox looked at the obsession in his time with economics and utilitarianism, and suggested the need of people like monks to be praying presences, whose concern was not to make money or to be useful, but to give glory to God. He showed how in history it has often been people who were praying, the great religious orders, who had offered the most effective ministry to the poor. He pointed to the fact that the monastery and the needs of the poor met at the monastery gates, where prayer and practice connected. In this boundary encounter there could be a transaction not just of handing out food to those who came to the monastery gates, but the giving of prayer and love in an exchange and partnership which was spiritual as well as material.

As these two movements developed, one about penitentiaries for people who had fallen and needed raising up, and the other advocating the valuable contribution that could be made by the organised religious life, Carter was already pursuing both possibilities. By the time Armstrong was writing his articles and the Rector of Morley had produced his book on monasticism, Carter and Clewer were already engaging on each of these fronts. By being upstairs enough they were learning to see through new eyes.

Fallen Women
He and his curate began by visiting in the terrible slum areas. They recognised the extent of the need and the particular problem with prostitution. One of the parishioners was called Mariquita Tennant. Typical of many women of that time she had been twice widowed and she was in her thirties. Mortality was very high. She had been married to the Anglican Chaplain in Florence – a priest called Robert Tennant. Rich Victorians travelled extensively in Europe and Florence was a popular place to visit. Tennant came to see the need to establish a house for 'fallen women' while he and Mariquita were in Florence. In that context he was particularly concerned for those who were "kept women". It was not unusual

for male travellers to take a woman with them on a trip to Florence, but then fall out with them, or simply meet somebody else. The original 'companion' was simply discarded. Such women would have no resources or connections and were left destitute, not knowing the language and therefore extremely vulnerable. As the Anglican Chaplain to the English people living in Florence, Tennant came across a distressing number of cases. Something similar happens to girls who come to this country for a better life and become trapped in slavery.

Mrs Tennant came back to Clewer when her second husband died, because her family owned the house next to the church. Living next to the church, having been inspired by a husband who had a vision of helping women who were discarded after having been sex slaves, she then encountered Carter and his work of engaging with similarly abused and needy women within the local parish. The problem can be highlighted by some statistics from the 1851 census. 559 people were living in 69 dwellings in one area. Besides such terrible overcrowding there was also an army barracks in Clewer. Many of these young conscripts were single people. Further schemes to bring the railway into Windsor involved the presence of 'navvies', who were seen as an additional moral threat, and there were many unlicensed beer houses (brothels) within the parish. These factors provided a formula for the exploitation, especially the sexual exploitation, of vulnerable girls and women in the locality.

As Carter and his helpers began to identify 'victims' Mrs Tennant took two or three girls being rescued from prostitution into her home. The first 'penitent' was rescued in December 1848, and within four months eighteen were housed under what Carter called 'her most hospitable roof'.[4] This was at a time when wider discussions were still seeking to crystallise the penitentiary movement into a public strategy. It is noteworthy that more women wanted to come as the word spread that help and rescue was available.

We can note a not unfamiliar pattern in parish life: it was not the vicar who started this offering of shelter, it was one of his parishioners who began providing space to help these women who were victims of the sex trade. Inevitably, Mrs Tennant found that she could not cope on her own. She was a highly strung person and some of the girls and women were alcoholics and difficult characters. They would shout at her and behave badly – they were not model guests. They had come into a "nice" home after having been on the streets living in very different circumstances. The story is a classic example of how we try to fulfil a vocation to help people in need – by doing the right thing - but without understanding the broader complexities, and thus not having adequate expertise or resources. Often this first step can be perceived as making matters worse – magnifying the problem and highlighting the inadequacy of current responses.

This very first community, in a house next to the church, became a place for slanging matches and screaming. Today we are more aware of the traumatisation of 'victims' of slavery. I will never forget meeting a Thai woman in London who had responded to an invitation to work in a restaurant, but was actually put in a brothel. She had been raped ten times a day. When she managed to escape, and I met her through an organisation that was supporting her, she had been so brutalised that she struggled to trust in the possibility of being human. We can imagine the dynamics of this house in Clewer when people rescued from such a brutalising environment were suddenly expected to live in a well-ordered home with a lady who had some status while in Florence with her clergyman husband. Too often the first steps of response can be in what turns out to be the wrong direction. There is a constant need to 'live upstairs' and seek further wisdom.

Organising Initiative

Carter had been called into a role of leadership in his community. He could see the issues and also the compassion being raised in the hearts of his parishioners. There was an urgent need for the response to be organised much more professionally. He gathered people to be trustees, and funds were raised to enable the purchase of a property. There was now the opportunity to provide proper resources rather than simply adjust existing domestic arrangements. One of his clerical friends offered to help in the parish for a limited time and he arrived with his recently widowed sister-in-law — a lady called Harriet Monsell who was forty years of age. Again a relatively young woman who was also widowed. In later years Carter reflected that it is important to look out for who God sends as possibilities unfold. First, there was the unlikely widow Mrs Tennant, who brought a partial vision and set an example of trying to respond. Then Harriet Monsell arrived on the coat tails of a relative and she was to prove to be the key to helping him see what was possible and then to design effective ways of delivering it.

Sister of Mercy

She began by assisting those who were trying to maintain the provision of care following Mrs Tennant's resignation on health grounds. Previous efforts were embraced. On 29th May 1851, Ascension Day, Carter admitted Harriet Monsell and clothed her in the church of Clewer as a Religious Sister - a Sister of Mercy. The word 'mercy' is very important — mercy not penitence. A more recent example would be the instinct of Pope Francis to ask for a year of mercy. Mercy is a very powerful word for a needy world. Carter made Harriet Monsell a Sister of Mercy. By this means she and the church declared a commitment to these needy women and girls, and to the work of rescue and restoration – through a particular value.

But the 'setting apart' for this kingdom work was also an expression of a commitment to the continuing need 'to be upstairs'. A commitment to the religious life involves the practice of a rule of life, with regular daily prayer and other disciplines to keep a focus on heaven, in order to see what is happening on earth more clearly.

Then, on 30th November 1852, St Andrew's Day, Harriet was professed as a Sister of Mercy in the presence of Bishop Wilberforce and installed as the first Superior of the Community of St John Baptist. By this time she has been joined by others seeking to participate in this commitment to live in heaven and work on earth through a religious community and a framework of spiritual discipline. Her own commitment now included inviting others to share in the work of mercy, and to oversee the resulting community. These events point to a very important model. Harriet Monsell is called as a woman, to lead a project for the wellbeing of women, and to pursue this by working especially with women. It is important to consider whether this was a typical 'Victorian' approach to care, as a female calling, or was this strategy pointing to something important about the place of gender in designing an appropriate response. It is also worth noting that St Andrews day was the anniversary of the consecration of Bishop Wilberforce, and whenever possible he spent this day at the House of Mercy – an important identification of oversight with outreach.

Practicing Partnerships

Characteristically Carter was in the background as the vicar, enabling these developments to happen. This was not simply a parish project – the parish acted as host, and offered support but the focus was clearly upon the people in need (not the parish being a smart organisation). Partnerships were emerging around the calling of persons and the developing of structures. Carter, Mrs Tennant and Harriet Monsell all played important but essentially complementary parts – making room for different gifts and contributions, learning from mistakes or inadequate pathways, and ever seeking to be bonded between themselves and with others in a deeper commitment to 'living upstairs' as a way of operating more effectively on earth. Others became attracted and involved – both as trustees/supporters, and as penitents/victims. At the heart of this initiative was a community of prayer – a 'religious community' embracing those seeking to deepen commitment and discipleship, and providing a gate for encounter and nourishment for those in need seeking support.

The Role of the Church

The person who wrote the first history of the Clewer Sisters was a scholar-priest called Donald Allchin. He commented that: "Clewer became the largest of the Victorian communities and in many ways the most influential. From the beginning the community was blessed with friendly Bishops."[5]

What he highlights is that it was not just Carter and the parish. This particular place was part of the Church's wider responsibility too. The Bishop's role in coming to pray for and bless Harriet Monsell, was a sign that this enterprise was inescapably part of the whole gospel for the whole of society. A truly kingdom enterprise. Whatever happens in a particular place is always a sign of what the gospel is about in the society in which it is set. This sign is to help other people to understand the message of the challenge, the needs, and the possibilities for responding.

Order and Structure

An important issue was the fact that Bishop Wilberforce was rather wary of religious orders. Many contemporaries thought that they were too Catholic. The Catholic hierarchy was only reintroduced in the middle of the nineteenth century after having been abolished in the Reformation. Two of Wilberforce's brothers became Roman Catholic, as did his sister – all children of William Wilberforce the great Anglican crusader against the slave trade. Further he was Bishop in the Diocese which provided the cradle for the Oxford Movement and a recovery of the Catholic Tradition in the Church of England. Many elements of this movement were initially dismissed as 'Romanising'. But Wilberforce also 'lived upstairs' and he could see that this initiative at Clewer was part of the DNA of Anglicanism. Although the Reformation process had limited some of these expressions of church in England in the sixteenth century, the time was now right to reconnect with this broader spirituality and its commitment, through leaders such as Pusey, to the needs of the poorest. Similarly, as Pusey also recognised, the monastic tradition always has a part to play.

By 1855 Bishop Wilberforce was back at Clewer blessing and opening the 'gate' of the new buildings. Serious structures for spiritual discipline and for daily living were being established. Committed prayer engaging with terrible need and oppression. In just three years there were eight sisters professed and thirty penitents living in the community. It is important to note that the community consisted of penitents and the community of Sisters living in relationship. An enactment of the complexity of our spiritual and personal formation recognised by Carter in the small group at the foot of the cross: the penitent, the distant relative, family and friend. This mix is important to own within each of us, but also within the dynamics of the groupings and partnerships we are called to both construct and 'consecrate'.

Bishop Wilberforce consecrated the buildings. There was a kitchen, a dairy, classrooms, and living quarters. One of the ways that the enterprise was sustained was by taking in laundry from the better off people who lived in Windsor. It was an offering of labour partly in the service of others — owning connectivity — but also a means of being more self-sufficient.

Earthing Priorities

Something worthy of note at this fragile, early stage of fashioning a response to the evils of slavery, is that despite a proper consciousness about 'living upstairs' — the agenda of heaven, nonetheless the first priority was very earthy — the provision of buildings, for accommodation, the laundry and classrooms. By contrast, at this stage of an initial consecration, there were only plans for a chapel. They did not build the chapel first because they could in fact pray without a chapel. Eventually a chapel was built to be a focus for prayer and worship together. But heaven is entreated for the sake of the present needs: on earth as it is in heaven. The practical priority of the reality of incarnation was the provision of structures to enable a viable life together. This project was about mercy.

A good gospel illustration of the dynamics of mercy that helped to inspire this Initiative was the story of the Good Samaritan — who showed mercy to a fallen person. The way the Good Samaritan showed mercy to a fallen person was not just to help them up, but it involved setting up a system. He found some money, he paid the Innkeeper - he set up a system to house and provide for a viable future of recovery and restoration. This was mercy in action. His prayers turned into action by taking money out of his pocket to create a real system, in a real place. Such a 'system' was the model for the Clewer Initiative. Resources for the more directly 'spiritual' nourishment of those involved could be developed later. Not least because religious resources carelessly constructed easily create boundaries and blockages that inhibit the work of the kingdom coming on earth. The 'religion' that seeks to nourish this common human spirituality needs to know its place – as doulos not master.

Attitude Shapes Action

What the Good Samaritan showed was that the key is not just a concentration on action, but rather an emphasis on attitude. The Samaritan acted out of mercy because of his attitude towards the person who needed mercy. His attitude was that this person needed caring for, and providing for, and he felt called to try to enable the action of mercy. This perspective of living in heaven creates an attitude that is then expressed in right action. Too easily in the church we can tend to concentrate on doing some good things and then pray about them subsequently. The wisdom Carter and his colleagues understood was the foundational importance of cultivating the attitude that makes it natural and instinctive in all of our relationships to act out mercy, especially when people are in helpless need. The Samaritan became a key example of this kind of gracious goodness.

Early in his ministry Carter had recognised that the inner life which the Bishop called 'living upstairs' was very important. It was key to being able to recognise the perspective of heaven which illuminated our earthly journey and helped people to see what is possible, while also providing the right attitude. He also realised that this same spiritual transaction was possible not only for the women who made up the religious community, but also for the women who came as penitents. They too could learn to see that larger vision and be graced with the attitude which would translate into the actions of charity - amongst themselves and through their witness into the wider community.

What is remarkable – and this set of developments is, of course, pre-Freud and what we now know about counselling and psychology – is that Mrs Tennant had had a taste of what a dangerous thing it was to have all of these women in one place and to try and treat them as 'normal'. They had been traumatised and were in a much more testing state. Today we are much more aware of 'trauma' and the role of therapy. Yet to our modern way of privileging counselling and therapy as 'scientific skills', it is a salutary challenge to consider this early strategy of prioritising the value of being part of a praying community as an essential resource.

Calmness and Confidence

There were offices during the daytime and a clear 'living upstairs' attitude as well as occupations such as the laundry. There was spiritual counsel and pastoral care, but as part of a call to penitence before the mercy of God, and the creation of a praying community seeking the attitude of grace that issues in acts of mercy. This strategy and structuring created a calmness and a confidence that indwelt people, though some failed and went back to prostitution or drink. Such unevenness was inevitable. The human context is that of the continuing limitations of an imperfect world and no institution can create a perfect solution. But Carter and his colleagues had begun to evolve ways of making significant progress in terms of tackling one of the key symptoms of sin and wickedness in their particular society. An important element was for each of the characters involved to develop the confidence to ask questions – of the self, of society, of the Gospel, of God. The questions provided the means of opening up individual vocations, the calling into being of partnerships, and the nourishing of a common attitude that connected all concerned with the acting out of mercy towards those in greatest need. The kingdom comes, and the Body of Christ is formed through this way of mercy – given concrete effect in a House or Household of Mercy – a living partnership nourished by grace and operating through faith.

Endnotes

[1] T.T. Carter: Sermons, Longmans 1875.

[2] V. Bonham: A Joyous Service: The Clewer Sisters and Their Work CSJB 2012. I am particularly indebted to the wisdom and scholarship of Valerie Bonham.

[3] Ed. W. H. Hutchings: Life and Letters of T.T. Carter, Longmans 1903.

[4] T.T. Carter: Harriet Monsell, Masters 1884.

[5] A.M. Allchin: The Silent Rebellion, SCM 1958.

4

A House of Mercy

For Carter the unfolding of the Clewer Initiative was a basic expression of the mission of the church – the invitation and engaging presence and power of the Gospel of Jesus Christ. Too often there is an assumption that mission is talking about God. In a way that seems logical, but if we look at the New Testament, Jesus does not simply talk about God. Those who talked about God were the Jewish leaders and teachers who thought they knew God and could instruct other people. That is often the impression of religion that comes across to those outside – some people knowing God and telling others what they should know about God too.

Father and Family

What is challenging to this stereotype, is that Jesus does not talk about God very much, He talks about a Father. This is a much more intimate and inclusive message about being related to God and to each other. More indirectly Jesus talks about sowing seeds, bad backs, people who are blind and fallen women who wash His feet. Jesus shows us that God's grace – mission being to share God's grace – and the miracle of the Christian gospel is among us, in us, between us, and is a force for good in our world. The gospels say that mission is about 'evangelion' — a word which means good news. Mission is not about an offer of access to a place of superiority or of spiritual privilege, but an invitation to acknowledge the connecting commonness of grace — the power and the presence of the Father in His children. The way that Jesus Christ does mission and shows the Christian gospel is in this gentle, everyday manner through which grace can be recognised and accepted as being present in our world to help us when we are hurting, give us confidence for the future and to enlighten us to recognise the miracle that God is in us.

Mercy

Carter understood this enlightening mystery very deeply. Of course, there was a Christian witness to be made, about knowing God and praying to God, but the primary manifestation of the gospel was through compassion: mercy. Through being gentle, gracious, taking people seriously and enabling their hearts to be more open to the power and presence of God to transform them and give them confidence and hope. The word Carter used most frequently was 'mercy'.

Mercy is a quality and a power that people easily understand — whether or not this is recognised within an established faith framework. In the work of rescuing and relating to the 'fallen', experience of those enslaved, their conditions, pains and pressures raised an instinct for compassion — an attitude expressed in reaching out to connect in the enacting of mercy. Mercy rises in human hearts and when people gathered in the various groupings that became the Clewer Initiative, the common force was the compassion which issued in acts of mercy, illuminating God's presence and power.

Rescue

There was a great deal of what was called 'rescue work' in the nineteenth century. Prostitution was an enormous problem and led to horrendous abuse of women, who had limited security or legal rights, and thus became easy prey to be drawn into the sex trade. The rescue work which developed in response to this cruel business was based upon the strategy of seeking to take the 'fallen' women out of the place where they were sinning – the sex trade – and then to place them somewhere else where they would be away from temptation, such as in service in a large house, so as to give them employment and a better environment. What Carter soon realised was that the key to effective rescue and rehabilitation was not simply moving victims from one situation to another, but more to enable them to taste mercy in their fallen state and thus to be nourished in their own sense of identity and being included, so that they might more easily learn to live in God's mercy, able to become in themselves agents of God's mercy too.

Reconnection

The aim was not to simply help them move from a bad place to a slightly better one but, rather to enable them to be graced, to grow and be blessed as the precious person each had been created to be. This reflects Wilberforce's reflection that Carter "lives upstairs" that is, if we look up to heaven and raise our sights then we can begin to see and experience mercy. Engagement in a religious community provided a taste of the mercy which opens up the path to being forgiven. Otherwise the pain and guilt of those who had been trapped in the sex trade too easily remained a crippling burden. Today with our understanding of trauma we may be more aware of psychological damage. Clewer was distinctive in recognising these deeper issues and offering a more personal, spiritual, healing response.

Housed in Mercy

One key ingredient was a suitable physical structure. The first step was to raise funds so that there was accommodation to provide a House of Mercy. This was only possible because of Carters strategy of involving other allies with a variety of skills and experiences. He persuaded the Provost of Eton and other key community leaders to contribute. Another ally was the Dean of Windsor. Similarly, Harriet Monsell had connections with politicians, landed gentry and church leaders – she was a cousin of A.C. Tait (Archbishop of Canterbury 1868-1882). All these allies could support the gospel of mercy and respond to schemes for turning this attitude into action.

Expanding the Offer

On a much smaller scale Carter encouraged people in the parish to support this provision of the basic structures for the house of mercy. Also, some of the women who joined the Community brought financial resources that enabled an expansion of the buildings and of the work.

As this alliance of partners and participants strengthened, resources were accumulated and further development included an orphanage and a convalescent hospital. Once people work together with mercy it flows more freely. We see the same process in the gospel as people meet the Lord. An example clear to Carter was the Samaritan woman who encountered grace in Jesus and then went back to her whole community to draw out this faith in goodness, which, as always, was more easily recognised when it could be consciously focused upon our Lord Himself. Compassion is the power that connects human hearts – but to be effective such 'alliances' need to be expressed tangibly, be supported by appropriate structures, and point to Jesus as the model as mercy.

Inexhaustible Sympathy

In his teaching Carter used to talk about the inexhaustible sympathy of Jesus Christ.[1] However difficult the situation might be, however bad the sin or reputation, Christ began His response with mercy, something Carter termed 'an inexhaustible sympathy'. That is the gentle gospel which tells those feeling vulnerable and in need that they are not beyond redemption. This was true even for a woman caught in the act of adultery. She was told to sin no more - there are standards, it is always possible to do better, but mercy will enable this better possibility. Carter emphasised this gentle gospel of grace inviting the needy into a richer way of living, as a vital contrast to the caricature of a stern God who has already judged and decreed punishment. He bears witness to a Father who loves.

He preached a very interesting sermon about Jesus' family tree.[2] The point Carter made is that if we look carefully at that family tree, Jesus, God's pure mercy – the purest mercy in human form that one could ever find – emerges from a line which includes Rahab the prostitute, and David whose son is Solomon, born of the wife of Uriah through an illicit affair. The preacher challenged his hearers to consider something about the realities of human sexuality and its complexity. The presence of abuse, double-dealing, sexual exploitation and even an arranged murder does not prevent the emergence of the Christ – the Saviour of the world. This supreme act of mercy is the sign that nothing is beyond the goodness of God which human beings are made to recognise and give themselves into. The response to the fallenness of the women who were rescued was not a relocation from temptation, but an engagement for rekindling their connection with mercy to enable each one to take their part with every other sinner (or one who falls short) in sharing the new life of grace that can emerge for the complexities and challenges of every family tree.

Living Beyond Lust

Carter wanted to invite people to recognise that we all stand on common ground, and in a line of sometimes questionable attitudes and outcomes, and therefore always in need of mercy. He followed Augustine and his teaching in recognising that to designate human beings as fallen, is to own the reality that each of us is full of lust. Lust is the word Augustine employed. What is seen in Adam and Eve is the lust for knowledge and to be like God. This notion points to a deep reality about the human condition. For instance if I am hungry I will lust for food. I lust for all kinds of things everyday – we each have strong desires. One of the great challenges to us as human beings is to control desire within us, between us, and with other people. Carter sought to explore how mercy frees us from this tendency. Often lustfulness is trying to fulfil desire because of insecurity or short-sightedness: a sign of living in the immediate with only the self as a point of reference. By contrast, knowing that we live in Gods mercy and that we can be agents of God's grace, saves us from such a narrow kind of lustfulness and is the key to opening up a larger more connected and more communal agenda. Energy for the wellbeing of others, through which we find proper meaning and fulfilment.

Carter provided illustrations of how this broadening work of mercy can transform lives locked into the lustfulness of survival and self-fulfilment, by pointing to the hard fact that Jesus is most noticeable because He chooses to eat with prostitutes and sinners. Jesus enjoys household intimacy and He shares mercy and fellowship with people who are involved in damaging relationships. And because we are all on a continuum of being fallen but desiring mercy to free us and to heal us, then we need to stand together. In Jesus mercy issues in intimacy – genuine friendship expressed through eating and drinking together. Family trees transformed by new relationships. For Carter this put sin in perspective.

The Sin of Society

It was too easy for his Victorian contemporaries to say that fallen women were sinners and to imply that others were, by comparison, fine. Carter was very clear that we are all sinners, we are all fallen, and we are all lustful. Of course, there are degrees but because we are all sinners we all need mercy. He stated that the people so easily identified as fallen women, may be in such deep sin not because they have chosen to be worse sinners than others, but due to the way society puts them in a very vulnerable place. It may be the sin of society that is causing them to be involved in such damaging behaviours.

With so many people living in hovels, with whole families in a single room, the result was a total lack of privacy. Sometimes two or three families would be sharing the same space overnight. It was not surprising that there was little sense of boundaries for sexual behaviour. He argued that crowded conditions gave insufficient space to preserve the "veil of human decency". Sadly this is still true of many cities in the world. From such a perspective there is an almost irresistible temptation for those who feel trapped in such circumstances to seek any means of escape in order to try to taste a different kind of life. The reality so often turns out to be a shift from one oppressive environment to an even more damaging context. The 'family tree' within which those subjected to these pressures were living, so easily becomes replaced by an even more destructive set of experiences.

Social Structures and Values

This unfolding narrative does not make the 'fallen' necessarily worse sinners than others, and there may be mitigating factors that are too easily overlooked. Carter discerned the creation of conditions in society that so increased the degree of vulnerability that such outcomes were almost inevitable. There was an urgent need to look at the structures, priorities and values of society, and not simply concentrate upon judging and reforming those who were its victims.

Carter invited people to consider their own involvement in the creation of an ecology which led to so many women being pushed into prostitution. He reminded the Sisters, the penitents and his parishioners that there is no limit to the sympathy with which Christ's sacred heart yearns towards the fallen. Christ's mercy is especially for those who have fallen furthest. He also challenged those who may have created these conditions by setting the bar of faith so high that people thought it was not worth trying to be religious. Mercy was the key tool.

Tackling Demand: Not Blaming Victims

He was quite unusual in seeing that it was not just the women who were the issue, but rather there was a more serious problem due to the fact that only the women were blamed for this sin. He commented about the men involved – the purchasers of sex: "the partners of her sin pass in and out amongst us unnoticed, save by the sleepless Eye of God."[3] The men who participated in this sin pass in and out amongst us unnoticed by the values and ways of 'the world'. But God notices.

In recent years there has been a movement to challenge this double standard more directly, very much along the lines Carter had suggested. In the Baltic countries, in France and in Northern Ireland, there has been a significant change in the law on prostitution. Traditionally it has been illegal to sell sex, but in the Baltic countries it is illegal to buy it. This is the crime which draws in the vulnerable to be exploited and abused. Carter witnessed this phenomenon in

Victorian society, although he did not get much of a hearing. He raised the sharp question - is the sin that of those vulnerable people who are involved in such wicked activities as the commodification and abuse of sexuality, or is it the sin of the people who are using their money or their power to create this market and draw people into it?

A Place for Prayer

To help pursue this agenda about sin, responsibility and mercy more fully, it was important to further develop the structures of the Initiative to provide a chapel. A dedicated space for seeking to learn to recognise, receive and reflect on the mysterious and life giving power of mercy. The chapel offered regular offices – structures for this spiritual work, and was designed to serve all of the elements of the growing communities. This included those called to be Sisters, as well as lay helpers and volunteers.

The key word was 'penitent'. The chapel was a resource for 'penitents' – though by this term he did not just refer to the obviously 'fallen'. Rather, Carter insisted that besides the victims needing to be penitent, the perpetrators needed to be penitent too, since this sin and lustfulness was creating the market. Further, the church needed to be penitent because of our neglect and failing to notice. Our collusion with indifference. Going even further, he called for a penitence in society for allowing these systems of abuse to develop and often to flourish, because of the prevalence of indifference or a false toleration.

Too easily 'church' becomes a narrow focus upon worship and fellowship, looking at sin in society from a distance. Then problems such as slavery seem essentially to belong elsewhere. Rather than simply blame 'society', Carter recognised that Christians begin, as he had in his parish, with seeking to grow within the Body of Christ. This is the place where mercy is really tasted and tested.

Confession

Because of this accent upon sin, falling short, and the need for the church to live and work by example, Carter valued confession. In the Anglican Church there has never been a requirement to go to confession, but there is an invitation if it might be helpful. Confession is where inner life and outer behaviour meet: but in Carter's time there was nervousness that confession was a papist practice. Carter wrote a book about the doctrine of confession in the Church of England.[4] He was clear that confession is not simply a means to improve a person's spiritual performance, but more profoundly it can be part of a process to enable the penitent to recognise their own fallenness, and from that perspective to seek reconciliation with God through His mercy. He highlighted reasons why confession could be helpful.

First because of our great liability to dishonesty – if we make our confession to God on our own there is a tendency to work within our personal comfort zones and thus not to be fully honest. Carter stated that sometimes the unseen presence of Christ needs to be made visible. If a penitent goes to a priest to say their confession, then in one sense the priest represents something of the physical presence of Christ.

Second, he argued that the humiliation of a confession challenges our pride and our self-sufficiency. There is some value in naming sin - not just generally but specifically. There is a humorous story of the little boy who went to confession and he did not know what to do. There was a card with a list of sins, to help people - so he just read out all of the sins and the final sentence "printed by

Mowbrays in London". It is not as simple as that, but naming the sin is important.

Third, Carter pointed to the value of being able to hear a caution and some reassurance of mercy and forgiveness. It is very difficult to hear the clarity of such good news on our own - the priest can give assurance of forgiveness and God's mercy. He recognised the danger in confession of the possible collusion of what was known as 'smoothing' – the penitent comes to know their confessor, who becomes a friend rather than a confessor. He advised people to read Psalm 51 "I acknowledge my transgressions, create in me a clean heart and renew a right spirit within me".

Overall he commended confession and as a result he received a great deal of criticism from those who were nervous about 'Catholic' practices in the Church of England. However his emphasis upon honesty, rigour and the clarity of God's assurance of grace was important. Moreover this spirituality of confession was a path towards being continually challenged to be more open to God's grace – a path which should be equally valuable to religious Sisters, parishioners, associates and 'penitents' (those rescued from slavery).

Dedication

On 1st July 1858 Bishop Samuel Wilberforce dedicated the House of Mercy. A sign that the Clewer Initiative had institutionalised compassion, with appropriate structures and a theological framework of humble attention to others, in order to better discern mercy, share it and work in it. Eight-hundred people came to the dedication of this House of Mercy - there was even a special train from Paddington. At this stage there were fifty penitents – women who had already been rescued. There was a council of nine clergy and nine laity and the Bishop oversaw the whole enterprise. There were also four trustees including Carter and Gladstone, the politician. Thus a wide range of allies bringing different expertise, contacts and vision. The whole structure which institutionalised compassion in this way was underpinned by the provision of an office book, based on the Book of Common Prayer and rooting everything in the prayer of the Church.

The House of Mercy held a number of vocations and spiritual journeys. There was a novitiate — a two year preparation to test a call to become a Sister of Mercy. This gave time for preparation, inner reflection, daily Holy Communion, regular silence and private prayer, alongside participation in the work of the Clewer project. Then there were lay Sisters who were perhaps less educated, but they came and worked in the institution. However these lay sisters were not just domestics - they made commitments, preceded by a novitiate of four years of preparation, in order to serve in this way. Further, there was a second order of Sisters. The full-time Sisters (the religious Sisters) and the lay Sisters committed to live in the institution as a religious community — but the second order Sisters lived at home for part of the year — being in fact a part-time member of the religious community. A model which is flexible and very Anglican! From 1855 others were invited to become associates as a framework for offering occasional help. Associates could be male as well as female, and this provided yet another model for commitment and involvement. Finally there were the penitents themselves, some of whom became 'Magdalens' — after Mary Magdalene — committed to full-time roles of working in the community, with a novitiate of seven years. Each of these ways of showing commitment and connection illustrates the practical and imaginative approach that was adopted to keep the Clewer project developing as a genuine 'initiative', open to the grace of mercy and flexible in response to the needs and sufferings of the vulnerable, as well as to the gifts and callings of those exploring how best to support this work.

Mortification

Besides a common framework of worship through their daily offices, Carter invited all of those involved to give serious consideration to the formative discipline of what he called 'mortification'.[5] He talked about how Jesus mortified Himself in regard to the love of home; He limited His enjoyment of that blessing. Similarly Jesus limited His attachment to place, He mortified Himself from creature comforts and He was often in the wilderness. He mortified Himself from having space for His own comfort. His life was always invaded by the crowds. In Jesus Carter saw a model of someone who in nineteenth century language practiced 'mortification' — i.e. limited what He wanted and could have, in order to create space for God and for others. The world was not simply to be reshaped for his own benefit, but rather the priority was reshaping for the wellbeing of others.

Carter tried to teach the Sisters, the lay Sisters, the associates, and the penitents that mortification was an important foundation to enable each of us to own our sinfulness and our need for mercy and grace. Mortification created space over against the lustfulness of the self, to enable a greater openness to God's grace. This was a theme of a number of his sermons to the parish and to the community.[6] Mortification was an indication of a serious attempt to step back from self and to create space for others, within the common and connecting grace of God's mercy. In this sense mortification helped to open the floodgates of compassion upon which the Gospel of Jesus Christ is founded.

Mortification was a discipline for each creature to create space for God, for others, and for the mercy of God's grace to begin to make us better connected for the fullness of the kingdom, rather than succumbing to the temptations to concentrate upon our own agendas – a salutary perspective for any Christian project.

Endnotes

[1] T.T. Carter: Spiritual Instructions: The Life of Grace, Masters 1883.

[2] T.T. Carter: Mercy For The Fallen, 1856.

[3] W. H. Hutchings: Life and Letters of T.T. Carter, 1903.

[4] T.T. Carter: The Doctrine of Confession in The Church of England, Masters 1865.

[5] T.T. Carter: The Imitation of our Lord Jesus Christ, Masters 1860.

[6] T.T. Carter: Spiritual Instructions: Our Lord's Early Life, Masters 1895.

5

The Pursuit of Partnership

Sustaining Commitment

All of those who became involved in this Clewer Initiative needed resourcing for the spiritual journey not just to raise up compassion in their hearts for people they found in need, but to make that compassion sustained, reliable, and effective in the society in which they were set. The Initiative flourished and developed because it was driven by a particular spirituality: the Holy Spirit of God and the coming of the kingdom.

The importance of carefully designed resourcing of this nature is to guard against the confusions of a less reflective response. The point is clearly illustrated by the fact that most of us are pretty generous in giving money to a one off cause, but this is a very different response to that of engaging with the real issues in society and being committed to a certain lifestyle, with institutions and structures to enable a sustained and effective effort. This challenge links with the observation about Carter by his Bishop, Samuel Wilberforce, who said "Mr Carter is often upstairs". The Bishop was drawing attention to the fact that his mind was searching to be drawn into the presence, power and purpose of God so as to better inform his witness on earth. That is why worship, confession and mortification became so important to the emerging of this enterprise. There was a continuing need to resist the temptation to reduce core concerns and priorities to more self-centred desires, supplemented by occasional acts of charity.

The first opposition to the Initiative was from those concerned that the church was moving from its proper field of religion and spiritual exercises, into the world of social work and politics, which was best left to others with more appropriate expertise. Carter recognised the dangers highlighted by this kind of challenge and he was always clear that a grounding in the humility of worship, confession and mortification would keep this Christian contribution focussed upon creative engagement with the needs of the most vulnerable, rather than in assuming responsibility for wider policies and performance. Nonetheless he clearly recognised that the models developed by the church for restoration through inclusive community had a great deal to contribute to the important debates of the times about values, priorities and good practice. This perspective honoured the paradox that there were no simple answers, but nonetheless committed people were called to offer signs of better ways of reaching out to the excluded and modelling richer forms of connectivity between different elements within a society.

Models of Re-Formation

Of especial importance was the Initiative's presupposition that the horrific abuse of the sex trade and associated alcohol issues were not simply the result of the failings and fallenness of the 'victims'. Rather the issues and appropriate responses involved all elements of a society – as the structures of the Clewer project indicated. All their endeavours were supported by the parish and the wider church.

This approach would enable women to be properly rehabilitated and to become contributors to the flow of mercy in their own right, rather than mere recipients of 'charity'. It also provided material and models for the on-going reformation of society.

Thus the heart of a Christian response was the creation of a network of complementary, but very different 'communities' – Sisters, lay Sisters, associates, penitents – all joined in a place of love, care and affirmation. There was no attempt to impose, control or focus upon just one group. The aim was to make new wine – though, like Jesus at the wedding at Cana in Galilee, everyone tasted the wine - not just the apparently respectable people. The Initiative recognised that new wine had to be available in abundance for everyone involved. This included having the courage to make the counter cultural statement that the penitents were not responsible for a particular problem called prostitution – rather every element in society had a part to play in diagnosing the real issues and in contributing to the crafting of appropriate responses.

The Role of the Vulnerable

Those who are vulnerable with multiple needs easily become dominated, and compliant in the operating of the abusive systems, whereas in fact Carter, his parish, and the St John Baptist Community were trying to honour the springs of grace within 'victims', and to enable this indwelling mercy to be part of the grace within other actors and agents – all for a common good, and depending upon being joined in a common humility. All are called to live by knowing a need to be forgiven and to seek the grace of God.

The whole project had started in a widow's house. A widow who herself was a vulnerable woman with limited legal rights – no man to look after her, discriminated against but yet helping other women. The first response was too complex for that little house and so others joined to help build bigger accommodation and a new household called a religious community.

Initiative Increases

In Jesus we see a similar shift from a home – that of Peter's mother-in-law, which became overwhelmed by the need of those turning up for help, to the calling of the twelve, the gathering of the women, the sending of the seventy-two and then at Pentecost the response of three-thousand. The kingdom project expands through different iterations - but all in the same spirit, the same mission. The same kingdom coming at every point. This is what happened with the Clewer Initiative. The spirit in it became contagious. An increasing number and variety of people were called, around the challenges of a basic need, but moving into a wider and more complex perspective and set of possibilities.

New Forms of Community

Carter tried to identify that spirit in people and find ways of it being nourished. Of particular importance was his recognition of the fact that with urbanisation the parish system in the nineteenth century was breaking down, and as a result more and more people did not know the church or have contact with any of its activities. Carter realised that besides a parish where people came to the local church, there was an urgent need for other forms of religious community. The Clewer Initiative was a particularly significant model for making religious community in a new and flexible manner, by people becoming nuns, lay Sisters, penitents, associates, trustees or supporters in other ways, all around a particular project for social justice – the greater inclusivity of grace. This provided an early example of how the parish system can be invited to thrive alongside other emerging networks for grace and goodness. A crucial factor, for Carter, was the purpose of such alternative communities, and their need to be placed creatively within the parish system. An interesting insight for our age of pioneering alongside more traditional parish ministry.

Connected in Charity

The key was a spiritual discernment to discover the common call – of the local church to serve the parish, and the Clewer Initiative to serve a certain section of particularly needy people within the parish. The fact that for a number of years Carter was both parish priest and Warden of the Community of St John Baptist is a significant example of this essential overlap and connectivity being modelled. Such a reality pointed to the fact that the spiritual needs and nourishment to be discerned and developed were common – but there needed to be different approaches to pursuing them. The parish had a universally recognised structure of priest, curate, churchwardens, officers, pastoral care outreach and a number of clubs and activities to support and grow different groups within the widest community. However the very strength and comprehensiveness of such structures had tended to provide patterns of ministry which concentrated upon refining and renewing the core activities. The value of the Clewer Initiative was the opening of radically new perspectives – especially the position of the abused as models for participation in the Body of Christ – as penitents knowing their need for peace – rather than as being seen to be simply a dysfunctional element needing spiritual 'formation' and restoration. The 'poor' were a gospel benchmark and indicator about the spiritual health and journey of the whole community. The work of the parish and of the Initiative complemented each other.

The presence of the convent, and associated enterprises such as the laundry and the orphanage, became an important sign to the parish, and to other parishes in the wider church, of the deeper dynamics of the Gospel of Grace and the spirituality of the Beatitudes. This was reinforced by the personal involvement of the Diocesan Bishop.

Calling for Health

In 1866 Carter preached a sermon about Jesus as the physician.[1] The point he made was that when we call out there is one who hears. He highlighted the most dramatic example, which is when Jesus calls out on the cross "my God, my God, why have you forsaken me?" and there is One who hears and in three days brings a resurrection. Carter stated in this sermon 'The more you call out the more He comes'. The more we call out to God the more the kingdom comes through His spirit, His power, and His presence. God comes into our heart and through our heart connects us with others, and suddenly we are not on our own. No-one is perfect but each of us can be with others on a common journey based upon owning a basic need for forgiveness, grace, and the support of others. Thus supporting each other.

That transaction 'upstairs' in our recognition of the common spiritual journey, brings empowerment 'downstairs' in Carter's language. And the commonness of our spiritual conditions creates the dynamic for recognising positively the connectedness of our earthly concerns and challenges. Thus the calling out for grace in our souls needs to be matched by connecting it to our calling out for health and wholeness for our bodies too. For Carter the more we call out together, the more effectively grace comes and meets us, catches us, embraces us, and encourages us. That was the experience of the Sisters in the community and it was the experience of the penitents. It was the root of parish life too. Part of such a common foundation for Carter was the bedrock discipline of confession and absolution. Only if there is real honesty about failings — a genuine calling out, can there be the fullness of response through which God can deeply touch us. When we have the courage to name our failings and call out for grace, mercy can be received.

Growing in Grace

Carter was clear that each of us is a person whose soul is formed to grow. Thus when we look at another person, the disciple is not to categorise them as fallen, a drunkard, a prostitute, or an enthusiastic vicar. What we see is a soul formed to grow in the grace of God. Carter was famous for writing liturgies. He wrote a particularly powerful liturgy for the reception of the penitent. The aim was to make somebody welcome when they arrived in this new place of community. Similarly, he wrote a liturgy for blessing a member when they left, and for consecrating somebody who was beginning to explore the spiritual journey more deeply. Each of these liturgies was a structure to let the cry of the heart have a focus and for people to be joined together in this cry seeking support for particular needs and concerns. The key was providing a structure of prayer and an opening of the scriptures. In these ways the praying cry of the heart was formed, and an atmosphere was created within which the soul could be fed, nourished and moved, not least in enriched appreciation of a wider connection with others. Such liturgies opened up participants to a greater sense of being blessed into the way of the kingdom — into a religious community in the fullest sense, embracing in the case of Clewer both the parish and the Initiative.

An example of his liturgical insight is illustrated in a prayer from one of these liturgies: "O Lord, Jesus Christ, who didn't suffer the woman from the city to kneel at Thy feet, and wash them with her tears, look favourably upon Thy servant, that being restored to the ordinances of Thy sanctuary, she may persevere in the ways of true repentance, may attain of Thee peace and a renewed life, and being cleansed from all her sins, may abide steadfast to the end, through Thy merits, Who with the Father and the Holy Ghost, livest and reigns forever. Amen".[2]

Unconditional Love

Carter and his colleagues recognised that before there could be proactive ministry to help 'penitents' own their need for forgiveness and new life, it was vital to invite them fully into the unconditional love of the Father – to own their creation and calling to be a child made for blessing and not for abuse or punishment. Today we recognise the danger of victims of slavery being re-traumatised by insensitive investigation or even through well-meaning small talk – both of which can trigger flashbacks and a crisis of self-confidence. Carter knew this truth about the delicacy of the abused person. While recognising the positive message that victims simply stand on common ground with all other children of God – as needful of forgiveness and mercy, he also acknowledged that the first task of a Gospel response is to build up the Body of Christ – in the individual as much as in the church.

Blessing

Hence his labours to provide frameworks for prayer and blessing from the very first encounter. The heart needs encouragement to cry out, and confidence that the cry is not only heard, but also elicits the response of mercy. The subsequent task of parish and religious community was to reinforce and nourish this primary spiritual experience of blessing. Similarly, the liturgy was central to providing this invitation and nourishment for all conditions and needs.

Thus, both in the parish and in the community of St John Baptist, everyone was invited to be caught up in the cry for blessing. This spirituality created a space in which each person could be touched by the grace of God appropriately, while further knowing that they were part of a kingdom project which embraced people for a wide variety of backgrounds and perspectives. Through this approach the journey and the location of each person could be taken seriously, in its precious uniqueness, but always as a part of a common, connected calling. In this way each person, and each place of discipleship becomes a potential site for mission, witness and learning.

Liturgical Prayer

What Carter helped to clarify amidst the testing challenges of his times, was that a structure of liturgical prayer could be the bedrock of a missionary outreach, and that the development of structures for such outreach needed to be imbued with the calling out for blessing. Such an approach created ways of worshipping, and of working in the wider community that became sustainable and rich in potential. In the parish and for the Clewer Initiative there emerged a sense of religious community where all of God's children are invited to cry out in their different places for God's grace to come and meet them together, and touch their hearts in a joining 'mercy'.

The Work Comes to Us

One of the things he wrote towards the end of his ministry, when he had been Warden of the Sisters for nearly fifty years is: "we did not plan the foundation of a Sisterhood and then seek work for it to do. The work came to us to be done, and a Sisterhood was the only practical instrument for carrying it on".[3] There was no analysis and then a plan to establish a religious community, rather energy was directed towards engagement with the real needs of people, in connecting with the power of God's spirit in their hearts. In articulating the cry of human hearts the spirit of God comes to meet, bless, grace, connect, and from this visitation of mercy came the recognition of a shape to receive such grace and structured ways of its being able to flourish. Christian ministry is to organise ways of God's grace flowing more freely into the needs and vulnerabilities of people's lives in a way that enables the widest possible tasting of that grace.

Endnotes

[1] T.T. Carter: The Life of Penitence, Masters 1867.

[2] J. Carter and W.H. Hutchings.   T.T. Carter, Longmans 1911.

[3] W. H. Hutchings: Life and Letters of T.T. Carter, Longmans 1903.

6

Hospitality

One of the drivers of Modern Slavery is the globalisation of indifference, and the extreme toleration which has been emerging from contemporary 'liberalism' — the granting of space to others which in effect severs any real interest in their choice of identity or its unfolding, for good or for ill. Children remain one of the few areas where this tendency is still recognised as inadequate and likely to open the way to abuse and harm.

In the nineteenth century there were fierce debates about the evolution of the liberal project in terms of the 'toleration' of differences. This was evident in the religious sphere, with greater legal rights and recognition being granted to nonconformists and Roman Catholicism. There were debates about the practice of religious tests at the ancient universities. In the political sphere there were moves throughout the nineteenth century towards an extension of the franchise and the clearer accountability of Members of Parliament to a greater range of citizens. In economics there was an increasing fascination with socialism as a tool for embracing differences in a more organised and inclusive framework. This was best illustrated by the development of Trade Unions — organisations creating particular markers around which to connect people in different places and roles. Markers such as wage levels and safety measures.

Within the Church of England the growth of difference in terms of styles of church making, especially in the Evangelical and Catholic Traditions, began to push the boundaries of what might be tolerated – with enormous resistance from those concerned with maintaining firm boundaries and clear distinctions.

Hospitality for All

Amidst these continuing controversies about the problems of 'difference' and the growing pains of what we have come to call a more universal understanding of toleration, Carter offered a completely different perspective. While fellow Christians took each other to court, and played leading roles in the many debates about 'toleration', Carter was clear about his own position in the Catholic wing of the Church of England. He articulated this with integrity, as in emphases upon confession and the fundamental foundation of liturgy. He held positions firmly, but with an engaging graciousness in relation to those of other views.

However his crucial witness was an insistence that Christianity was not about 'toleration' as an uncritical endorsement of whatever people seemed to desire. Nor was it about defending firm boundaries over against 'difference'. Rather, for Carter and the whole Clewer Initiative, what was primarily distinctive about the Christian gospel was hospitality.

An emphasis upon inviting people who are different into a common space and crediting them with the possibility of sharing goodness together. The key model would be that of the Last Supper. The people present included those who had betrayed Jesus – Judas,

Peter and others. Yet they were all invited to receive hospitality. This inclusiveness was the summation of a whole ministry, in this moment of hospitality. Similarly, in Simon the Pharisee's house Jesus draws attention to the fact that the hospitality should include the participation of a sinner, the prostitute from the city. Carter recognised the inclusiveness of the invitation to receive the hospitality of God's grace, which could bind people together in one Body (His life) and give them courage and hope to pursue goodness. He recognised that hospitality was the great sign of the gospel. A hospitality that is generous and inclusive of those who appear to be less deserving – a categorisation that generally coincided with those who were also most vulnerable.

Catholicity and Diversity

He observed that "the eye resents sameness …,".[1] In human terms the result should be that "each regard the other according to their several vocations, with mutual respect, and sympathy and love". Yet such diverse gifts were "not to exalt the individual, but to perfect the Body of Christ". A radical understanding of Catholicity.

This insight explains why the buildings and the liturgies designed to welcome and embrace women coming into the community and its outreach, emphasised their calling to be loved and blessed. The first message was to acknowledge not a person being abused, but a member of a community joined in prayer and learning - with God's love amongst them, and an integral part of the wider work of the church in society. The people who ran the community – the Sisters and the clergy – were sinners too. They all needed the same hospitality, which lifted them out of the things that divided them and so often tended to accentuate the differences that too easily bring damage.

Sexuality – Identities and Disciplines

A challenging example of this whole issue was the nineteenth century debate about celibacy. The women who were called to join the religious order began to ask if they could take vows, as in the traditional religious orders, of poverty, chastity and obedience. These were proven ways of bringing a community together – common obedience to a common rule. Since many religious orders were made up of single people trying to create a community, the issue of sexuality needed to be addressed, and chastity had early been identified as a helpful frame. In the background was the continuing Anglican anxiety about what were seen to be Roman Catholic practices, both vows for religious and the celibacy of priests. For these reasons there was considerable debate about whether or not the women should be allowed to take such vows. The Bishop of Oxford, Samuel Wilberforce, was nervous because of the implications of moving towards a more Roman Catholic way of structuring spirituality.

Carter was clear that he wanted to listen to what the women were saying in terms of being drawn together into a community to serve their sisters who had been suffering from the sex trade. He began to take seriously their request. The Sisters wanted to take vows of poverty, obedience, and also of chastity. These were partly traditional vows but Carter wanted to explore the spiritual need being expressed and the best way of shaping a common life and witness.

In 1871 the Bishop of Lincoln, Dr Wordsworth, stated quite boldly that nobody should be allowed to take a vow of celibacy who was under sixty years old. He was sixty-four when he made that statement! The Victorian attitude towards sexuality was very narrow. Carter could see that the women were asking to take vows in order to be better knitted together. He came to understand through working with them that they saw the vow of celibacy as confirming in them a spiritual gift to be joined together in offering hospitality to others – to the people in need who came to join this extended communion and to receive their love in a different way to the more sexualised expressions of desire which they had experienced.   Their commitment to their sexuality was to put that energy into being a hospitable community that could receive others who were suffering from the opposite extreme of handling sexuality through promiscuity and prostitution.

The Sisters wanted to show that there was a discipline which they could observe in a way that would be a positive expression of their sexuality, and a counter cultural witness to contemporary presuppositions. Vows would enable the Sisters to make a statement about themselves and their sexuality.   Carter came to recognise that marriage fulfilled a similar function and made a similar statement.   Marriage was a commitment about sexuality which created amongst other things, a community to be hospitable to others.   The Sisters living together were a larger version of that possibility.   They too wished for structures and commitments to better enable them to become a new community together facing out into the world.   Being bonded in the love of Christ in order better to offer love to others.

The modern marriage service articulates this image and reality: through their vows husband and wife begin a new life together in the community. The Sisters were seeking a similar kind of discipline about sexuality, which provides a resource to service the gospel emphasis upon hospitality in a world of destructive difference and selfish desire.

Discernment and Development

Eventually Carter persuaded Bishop Wilberforce and his successor to allow the gradual introduction of commitments which became in due course, more formal vows, in order to create this community of hospitality. The struggle was significant because for the Sisters, as acknowledged by Carter, it was in pursuit of finding appropriate ways to be better agents of God's mercy – God's hospitality to sinners. To achieve this call there was the challenge to own that they were all sinners, and then to find a way of accepting God's mercy and hospitality into their lives so that they could be agents of such grace to others. The debates and the discernment were 'held' within the framework of the various forms of spiritual direction that Carter had helped to evolve in order to take seriously each individual journey, while enabling a richer connectivity to the common calling.

A good example of his teaching about this kind of process of discernment comes from a course of preparation for Lent which he offered. He emphasised that the reflection of prayer should focus on the day.[2] The model from Jesus. "Give us this day our daily bread". It was important to pray for the day and trust God's grace for the next one. This is very difficult given our tendency and capacity to anticipate the end of the story and how it can be achieved. There needed to be more space for the enlarging powers of mercy.

Next he invited them to observe the hours – that is to pray regularly and use fixed liturgies that ensure a full engagement with the teaching of the Gospel. This is an important discipline to provide a clear framework within which more personal agendas and immediate schemes need to be tested and enriched. Third, Carter advised them to meditate on a grace. He suggested thinking about 'a grace' – something that would really allow God to bless the one praying and then for a whole day to meditate on it – the grace might be patience, perseverance or humility. The focus and cry of the heart provides an opportunity for more specific blessing to be received.

Fourth, there should be some devotional reading during the day. And at night it was important to recollect faults. He advised that when thoughts wander during prayer, it is helpful to make the sign of the cross, that is to do something physical to bring back a sense of focus. Lastly, on going to bed, the person should pray for rest.

This scheme displays his insistence upon seeking guidance rather than answers, and cultivating attitude as an essential precursor to any action. There is always more to seek and more to receive. A spirituality of trusting hopefulness – a model of the primacy of blessing which victims were invited to taste as the foundation for growing in wholeness.

Being Tested

Yet Carter himself was tested too. He was a committed high church person, at a time when there was great suspicion of Catholic practices. He had candles on the altar – a sign of the encouraging mystery of God's light. This was seen by the "hotter" kind of Protestants as being blasphemous and they took people to court for these kind of practices. The most famous example was the trial of Bishop Edward King in 1888. Similarly a Protestant gentleman, Dr Julius, who lived in Clewer, took Carter to court through an organisation called the Church Association – for what were called 'ritualistic practices' – including having candles on the altar and the use of vestments.[3] Radical Protestants could find no rubrics in the Book of Common Prayer to endorse such practices and felt that they were, therefore, an illegitimate development. The Bishop

of Oxford at that time, J.F. Mackarness, the successor of Samuel
Wilberforce, felt that he should hear this complaint, but it went
into the secular court system. The Bishop of Oxford contested this
process and said such issues were matters for the Bishop and the
Church, not for the secular courts. He lost the case but it went
to the House of Lords where his rights were upheld. It was the
responsibility of the Bishop to interpret the Book of Common Prayer
and the practices of public worship, not a judge in a secular court.
The Bishop of Oxford did not agree with these so-called 'ritualistic
practices' but because of his respect for Carter he was prepared
to leave the matter and not act on the complaint. That was an act
of hospitality and toleration of one of his clergy (Carter) with
whom he clearly disagreed.

Carter knew that the Bishop did not approve and thought it
would be wrong to take advantage of his hospitality, and so he
resigned. He was seventy-two at the time that he resigned. The
Bishop had not asked him to resign and had not told him to stop
the contested practices. But Carter felt that he should not accept
this generous kind of hospitality. He knew the Bishop's views and
felt that it would be a breach of hospitality to take advantage of
such generosity. Hospitality is about an active mutuality despite
differences. Carter felt that he should not presume on this
interpretation. The Bishop accepted his resignation and the next
day gave him a licence to be Warden of the Community of St John
Baptist. Somebody else became the vicar of the parish but Carter
remained as warden until he died on 28 October 1901.

Humility Overcomes Differences
At one level this is a story of holy people vying with each other
to be hospitable. In a world where we are quick to claim our
rights and criticise those with whom we do not agree, the

graciousness of hospitality introduces a very different dynamic. The Bishop indicated that he would not do anything even though he believed the practice to be wrong, while Carter knew that the Bishop held these views and thus was determined not to take advantage, but rather to be hospitable towards the Bishop. A strange picture of people trying to live with extra hospitality rather than claiming rights. Rather than indifference or uninterested toleration, there was a real concern about the other. The story highlights humble attempts to reach out across the differences, so that God's mercy might bring blessing at a cost to the person offering hospitality. A similar spirituality to that of the women who wanted to make a vow of celibacy, or a couple sharing this mutuality in marriage, - a desire to make a commitment to the other in order to create a hospitality which is primarily for the needs of those beyond. The desire is to discipline self for the sake of being able to widen the bounds of hospitality. Certainly the Sisters, under Carter's influence, were not taking these vows for themselves to be good, pure and holy, but rather to create a community of hospitality. In a similar spirit Carter and his Bishop put hospitality before personal preference and their particular Christian convictions, so as to facilitate the sharing of God's mercy across what could otherwise have become irreconcilable differences.

Overseas Expansion

Such hospitality in the service of mercy quickly creates good will, richer relationships and an outgoing energy. The mercy tasted in the convent was soon to spread into extensions of the Clewer Initiative in India and America. Several other branches developed in England too. Each was a further attempt to create spaces where the hospitality of God could be tasted and shared with others so that they too might know something of that abundance of mercy, which was such a primary sign of the coming of the Kingdom.

Protection Not Judgement

Carter offered some interesting teaching about how we see Jesus ministering this mercy to people who were sinners, which of course includes all of us. One of the instances he considers is the case of the woman who is taken in the act of adultery, which clearly was a sin.[4] There is recognition of a case of sexual misdemeanour but what Carter noticed is that the first thing Jesus does, is to protect the woman from the scorn and judgement of others. In a way He is hospitable to her, in her sin, because He takes her side against those driven by a simplistic approach to difference and judgement.

Priority For Potential

The law made provision that she should have been stoned. Instead Jesus gives her a space to have another chance. He has faith in her, indicating that there is something better and richer that she can become, the transgression notwithstanding. Thus the woman tastes forgiveness and can try again. Jesus says that He does not condemn her, but that she should sin no more, because He knows that she can do better. The sin has happened and if it is simply condemned then the sinner is locked in a dark place. Instead, Jesus does not ignore the sin but He is clear that there are greater possibilities for her. In His hospitality He says "sin no more, because in my company you are made for greater things."

Double Standards

Everybody else present in this scene is also invited to practice greater hospitality, by looking more critically at their undoubted rights to judge and to stone the woman. With deeper reflection, no-one present is sure whether they have the right to judge and condemn. They all go away. They each leave the scene of this meeting. They take themselves away because they realise their calling under God is not to stone this woman, who almost certainly would not have been a willing partner to the crime – as with Carter's penitents. It is significant that the man who had committed adultery was not present. The law stated that they should both be stoned, but in the way of the world, it was just the woman who is seen as the sinner. We have seen that Carter recognised that it was women who were blamed for prostitution, not men. Most of the people trapped in this abusive trade were poor, broken creatures, corrupted by male wealth and male dominance.

Yet a Common Cry

In the story Carter explored the fact that each person present is challenged to claim some of God's mercy for themselves through deeper reflection and by making space for difference. This kind of response created a hospitable place for Jesus and for the woman. Carter showed that this story illustrated the role of the religious order.   It was to be a hospitable place where people were rescued from prostitution, from the condemning judgement of others, in order to be given permission and encouragement to become more fully the person each had been made to be. They should be able to receive and respond to the call of God more directly. Those inclined to more decisive judgement of others had much to learn too – not least about their own need for forgiving people, and thus an acknowledgement of a common cry for mercy.

Generosity

The hospitality of God was often revealed in the midst of the trappings of sin and the condemning righteousness of human systems.   Carter recognised that the welcoming of women superficially accused of sexual misdemeanour into the merciful space of a religious order was an enactment of this Gospel story. Amidst all the necessary systems of law, rescue and restoration, there needed to be an absolutely crucial space for grace – for a forgiving, welcoming, encouraging mercy. The centrality of love for the most vulnerable becomes the litmus test and life giving energy for every attempt to judge, resolve or reform. In the fight against Modern Slavery, as with the original Clewer Initiative, the most powerful factor is this ministry of generous mercy – the commitment amidst all the professional systems to be there for people in their need and to show confidence in their future.

The Widest of Promises

When abuse has crushed the humanity and the hope in victims there is a deep need for the presence of mercy – the promise of unlimited grace. The administration of law always needs balancing in this way, so that schemes to identify and practice justice are grounded in the primacy of hospitality. Jesus tried to help the scribes and the Pharisees find a place of communion with prostitutes and publicans through the hospitality of table fellowship – a space for shared nourishment with a willingness to refrain from condemnatory judgement, to reflect more deeply about motes in our own eyes, and to give room for God to offer hope and grace for the uncertain futures of the most vulnerable.

Alongside the vocations of those who administer the law and the systems to create security, stability and important standards of behaviour, there needs to be the balancing, challenging contribution of this Gospel about the wideness of mercy and the hiddenness of much human potential. Carter clearly saw the role that the church could play, alongside legal and civic endeavours, to go beyond the more obvious demands for order and judgement, in a way that replaced such a division within society with acknowledgement of an underlying connectivity in the need for improvement, and in the mutual recognition of the possibilities in the unexpected and undeserved gifts of grace. Every contributor to the working of law, order and welfare, needed to reflect upon that paradoxical message: "I do not condemn you – sin no more".

Carter's work and teaching at Clewer insisted that everyone needed God's hospitality. None can have a monopoly of giving out hospitality – we all need to receive it.

Endnotes

[1] T.T. Carter: Harriet Monsell, Masters 1884.

[2] J. Carter and W. H. Hutchings: T.T. Carter, Longmans 1911.

[3] The Founders of Clewer, Mowbray 1952.

[4] T.T. Carter: Mercy For The Fallen.

– Sermons for The House of Mercy, Masters 1856.

7

Confronting Sin and Owning Evil

Carter's emphasis upon the priority of building up the Body of Christ when he first went to be the parish priest in Clewer provided the essential perspective and foundation for the Initiative which developed to offer a unique approach to the support of victims and the crafting of a more fulfilled future. As the Clewer initiative expanded through the structures of the religious order, the House of Mercy and a number of other ancillary operations, this bedrock of worship and space for reflection was maintained - and given priority in terms of daily offices, Sunday worship and the encouragement for each person to seek the benefit of spiritual direction. An ownership of the need for confession and absolution, and for participating in the life of the Body of Christ as sign and agent of the coming Kingdom. The challenges of their particular context, highlighted by the prevalence of prostitution and alcohol abuse, together with the continuing need of each individual for cleansing and renewal, were held within a structural commitment to gather in church or chapel to say thank you for the goodness and grace of God.

The particular pressures in society, in the various groupings within the parish, and in each person, needed both space for reflective prayer as a source of potential enlightenment and encouragement, and a continuing rhythm and repetition of the life of the church expressing the core doctrines of a Trinitarian faith through creeds, sacraments, scriptures and authorised teaching.[1] The lectionary and the calendar of the Christian year provided a particularly important resource to put more current issues and agendas in a deeper perspective - that of the life of the whole church, living and departed, expressed through these particular gifts of God.

The Reality of Evil

This immersion of current concerns and practices within the life of the church would, according to Carter, challenge Christians to recognise the reality of evil.[2] He saw that 'evil' was an important theme in scripture, and especially in the teaching of Jesus, not least in the Lord's Prayer. Yet, as is perhaps even more the case today, people were becoming less sure about the term, and tended to interpret events through a more human lens. There might be medical or social analysis to explain behaviour or attitudes that had traditionally been associated with demons or the evil one.

Messiah – More than a Model

The increasing focus in the nineteenth century upon the incarnation encouraged an interpretation of the person of Jesus as a model to enhance human being, rather than a Messiah who confronted the devil in the wilderness as a force aiming to undermine His ministry and offering an alternative sovereignty. Further, Jesus clearly challenged the demonic in people He encountered. St Paul was also clear about the reality of evil and the need to take this seriously in discerning the contours of God's call in a fallen world.

Sin – In Self and In Society

Carter held that to engage fully with scripture within the prescribed worship of the church was a discipline that would help us own and confront the depths of sin and the reality of evil. His emphasis upon confession and absolution was not aimed at enabling a process of 'fine tuning' for Christian lives – rather this practice invited a much deeper engagement with the reality of sin and the power of evil, certainly within the person, but more within the structures and relationships through which they were placed in a wider society.

Confession Clears the Way

Such an approach to the role of Christian worship ensured that all those involved in the Clewer Initiative were not simply trying to offer pastoral support to the vulnerabilities highlighted by the slavery rampant in the parish. Rather, recognition of the reality of slavery demanded an appeal to resources well beyond their own capabilities, and a paying attention to the sheer depth of the abusive depravity being organised - which is something too easily ignored or minimised by an understandable concentration upon pastoral practice and local organisational arrangements. To be involved in the Clewer Initiative was to be called to name sin, to recognise the reality of the forces of evil, and to know that without the gratuitous gift of grace there could be no real progress.

Further Carter reinforced this teaching by reference to the parable of the person cleansed of sin, whose life was like a house swept clean, and thus even more exposed to the indwelling of increasing forces of evil. There was never an easy security in the work and witness of the Initiative. Apparently tangible signs of 'progress' such as the dedication of new buildings and the growth in numbers of Sisters or penitents, needed to be handled with great care as markers on the spiritual journey.

Celebration and thanksgiving as responses to the goodness and grace of God should always be balanced by continuing self-examination together with the ownership of evil in the self, in the community and in wider society. This is one of the reasons that Carter became sympathetic to the Sisters' request to make the traditional vows of poverty, chastity and obedience. They were proven ways of highlighting the key areas within which sin and the power of evil operate - and there was a continuing need for vigilance, and a commitment to use this frame for examination, repentance and renewal.

A Dynamic between Light and Darkness

Carter pointed out that in creation there is a very basic rhythm between light and dark, day and night. The darkness is very real, though when it engulfs us we know in our faith that light and warmth is somewhere present and on its way to returning to us. The light and the warmth is always present but there will be moments of darkness, literally and metaphorically, as well as times of half-light and shadow. This complex of conditions is central to the spiritual journey. When there seems to be a preponderance of darkness or dimness we have to cling to the fact that we know goodness and grace is present, even if at this point we seem to be in the cloud. One of the great images that Saint Paul uses is recognition of the reality of only seeing through a glass darkly. There is never a state of perfect everlasting light. The sun does go down but the rhythm of creation for light to return can be trusted. We do not live in perpetual light, but we do not have to live in perpetual darkness. We can live knowing that through the cloud there is goodness and grace.

The Limitations of Experience

This perspective enabled Carter to be realistic in his teaching and in his oversight of the Clewer Initiative. He found that Christian people, through the miracle of tasting mercy, can easily be drawn into placing a huge emphasis upon 'experience' – especially what can seem like measurable outcomes to God's mercy. The danger of this approach is that it tends to put the individual or a particular group at the centre of how values and situations are measured or developed – because 'experience' is always limited to the capacity of those in the situation to understand or articulate what it might mean.

The Anglican tradition has been wary of 'experience' as a key director of the spiritual life, not least because of its tendency to move towards enthusiasm or despair – both emphases tending to serve as a further narrowing influence in making the focus of reflection and response relate to the particular, at the expense of the always broader call of the Kingdom. For Carter, as a priest deeply influenced by the Oxford Movement[3], the work of John Keble in producing an edition of the works of Richard Hooker was especially significant.

Hooker highlights the three key tools for Anglican theological reflection – scripture, tradition and reason. Each guarantees the primacy of God's greater agenda over the more immediate 'experience' of Christian disciples in a particular context. Scripture as the word of God and the teaching and calling of the Father. Tradition represents the accumulated wisdom of the Church, the summation of generations of Christian experience and reflections shaped and ordered for the wellbeing of the Body and its best functioning in worship and witness. Reason for Hooker, in the tradition of Aristotle, was not the human faculty to think and judge, but the mind of God which human beings are created to be able

to discern and in which to be joined together within His purposes
and priorities. Reason is the human capacity to share in the mind
of God, and thus a resource indwelling the church, not an
independent faculty in the individual.

Including the Excluded

For Carter these three tools gifted to the church were the essential
means by which human experience could be interpreted, shaped
and developed. Hence his prioritizing of keeping worship as the
foundation. This was a challenge to an increasing confidence as
society was becoming more 'plural' for the localisation of experience
to be the key to understanding identity and calling – for various
Christian 'groupings', as much as for those who pioneered the
impressive works of Victorian philanthropy. Carter's teaching, and
the development of the Clewer Initiative, valued both experience
in terms of social issues being faced, and the particularity of a
certain approach to worship (the Anglo Catholic approach) – but
he was clear in all his teaching that both of these inevitable factors
needed to be brought humbly and regularly before the judgement
of God. This discipline would enable the realities of sin and evil to
be owned, and blessing received in a way that would call out
reflection and response towards the new life of the Kingdom, the
abundance of mercy, rather than the simple reinforcement of
positions and perspectives apparently 'achieved'.

The foundation of worship under the discipline of Scripture,
Tradition and Reason was the key to being continually called to
participate in the proper catholicity of the coming Kingdom. The
measure being the inclusion of the excluded, rather than the
clarification or crystallisation of one's own 'experience'. This
approach was vital to a serious attempt to fulfil the Lord's call to
the service of others as doulos, slave of the Kingdom – rather than

servant of what might seem to be the obvious next stage in terms of the immediate context.

Beyond Our Small Worlds

Too easily human beings can be tempted to reinforce the security of a small world built around the positives of immediate experience – and thus to live in 'echo chambers' where current thinking and practice is ever magnified, but never developed further. This tendency is enormously encouraged in our contemporary society through our ability to change channels, delete and highlight 'likes' or 'friends'. By such means the 'material' that is the stuff of life becomes insulated from anything but a carefully controlled development – rather than open to radical critique, the recognition of the prevalence of sin and evil, and the openness to significant change.

The Limits of Desire

Carter explored these issues in his teaching about the Prodigal Son from Luke chapter 15.[4] The Prodigal centred all his resources upon reinforcing the experiences which seem to benefit his own life, despite some questioning reproach from the wider society. He indulged his own experience: it became the key guide to his behaviour and his values. In the terms of an earlier chapter, he pursued the passions of his own lust. The logic of this emphasis upon experience is that the individual will become totally isolated and alone – surrounded by others but disconnected from any common framework of values (Scripture), narrative (Tradition) or shared process of discernment (Reason). Values, narrative and thinking have all be subsumed in the service of his own experience.

In this dark and lonely place, the place which is simply that of his own experience and its inevitable bankruptcy, Carter noted that the boy's instinct is to call out for his Father. And when we call, as he had long taught, there is One more than ready to hear and respond. The Prodigal, faced by the limitations of the capacities of his own experience, is now glad to recognise that this 'personal' reference point is already embedded in a family, a culture, a set of potentially nourishing and caring relationships. Something that the Scriptures call a 'household'. In his case a household with a tradition of inclusive hospitality: "even the servants" are blessed by its workings. A household bound together by a more self-conscious participation in the presence and purposes of God (Reason).

Overcome in the Father's Love

The Prodigal was able to own the reality of sin, the presence of evil, as he composed his liturgy "Father I have sinned against you…" This step of humility, of calling out for mercy, moved him towards an encounter in which his fallenness and frailty are overwhelmed by the sheer generosity of the Father's mercy. "Bring the best wine" – "kill the fatted calf". He is not greeted by condemnation, but with a party. There is a clear underlying message – echoes of Jesus saying to the woman caught in adultery "I do not condemn you….sin no more". He is welcomed into the inclusive fellowship of the Kingdom community – a mixed household where the celebration is focussed on the new and better possibilities for which he has been made. The power of mercy turns the focus from his past towards his potential.

Connected in a Different Community

This is the power of the community gathering for a thanksgiving that recognises the darkness of sin and evil, and its root in an excessive emphasis upon human experience: and which then celebrates in order to provide the nourishment for putting that past behind him, so as to better enable him to play his part in the unfolding future of the Father's household. Since the real estate has been given to his elder brother, he would be able to participate as a doulos rather than as an overseer!

By contrast the elder brother was unable to own any sin or evil in himself – he was equally focussed on his own experience, as a servant to his Father, the subtle form of self-righteousness which so easily possesses Christian disciples. He was unable to enter into the liturgy of the Household, revealed by the Prodigal as beginning with confession: "Father I have sinned".

Body, Soul and Spirit

For Carter these insights pointed to the importance of the soul. He helped his parishioners and the community learn that to be human is to exist in three modes. First he used the word 'carnal' – or 'flesh' in the New Testament. Each person has a 'fleshly' existence, expressed through the importance of appetites. Second, each person is a soul, a way of being that transcends the merely physical nature of the flesh, and which needs a different kind of nourishment. The soul enables a person to rejoice, imagine, regret, know goodness and grace, and to reach out beyond the apparent confines of our more earthly experience. Yet the soul is part of the fleshliness of the body.

Thirdly, Carter pointed to the power of the Holy Spirit, which is God's presence and power and purpose, and can act like the sunshine to warm and lighten body and soul. The spirit can give power to the soul to enable engagement even with the powers of darkness and death. This indwelling of body and soul by the spirit gives Christians the confidence to face a bereavement with the prayer: 'may they rest in peace and rise in glory. The spirit touches the soul and enables the body to journey through death into resurrection and ascension.

Carter was keen for Christians to recognise these realities to enable a more insightful reflection on the pressures and possibilities of life – particularly as highlighted in the challenge of sex slavery and alcohol abuse in his own parish, as a sign of a serious issue in society. The issue pointed to the continuing abuse of the vulnerable and their exclusion even through many schemes ostensibly designed to help them.

Soul Sharing

His emphasis upon the ever present realities of sin and evil, the resources of Scripture, Tradition and Reason gifted to the church to help identify, confront and overcome such challenges, and the potential to grow in the Holy Spirit while body and soul remained in the continuing dynamics engendered by the fallenness of human being – all pointed towards realistic responses and the highest ideals regarding the possibilities of future blessing.

The Clewer Initiative was based upon the discipline of paying special attention to the life of the soul – seeking openness to the Holy Spirit while being rooted in the very real limitations of the body, especially the real presence of sin and evil. For Carter the soul was the space for spiritual engagement and the faculty through which goodness and grace could be received and shared into everyday life, so that sin and evil might be properly overcome.

Endnotes

[1] T.T. Carter: Parish Teachings: The Lord's Prayer and other Sermons, Masters 1886.

[2] T.T. Carter: The Life of Sacrifice, Masters 1864.

[3] T.T. Carter: Undercurrents of Church Life in the Eighteenth Century, Longmans 1899.

[4] T.T. Carter: The Life of Penitence, Masters 1866.

℮ ℮ ℮

8

Deep Cleansing for All

The Agony of Waiting

To trust in the wholeness of the work of the Spirit required the
courage to own our past in a creation that was characterised by a
'a groaning' for completion, while being confident that each small
step in our own lives could be a part of this vocational dynamic
through which the Kingdom was arriving. Carter tried to help
those involved in the Clewer Initiative to recognise the reality and
the inevitability of the struggle, and yet the significance of steps
that become signs of the mercy which meets our efforts becoming
enfleshed, as markers of progress and encouragement. In a series
of lectures for Lent, he explored this dynamic in the life of our
Lord.[1] The continual challenge of corruption leading to the cross,
and yet the equally tenacious signs of hope and wholeness,
culminating in the Resurrection. A pivotal point was the agony of
waiting while every hope seemed to be entombed in darkness and
death – with no notion that the stone which sealed this mortal
journey could ever be rolled away. In this agony of waiting and not
knowing it could seem to be most natural to live in mourning for
what might have been, a cherishing of memories, and a desire to
salvage some of the benefits which have been glimpsed.

More Voices

But for Carter, the importance of prayer, or the place where the soul owns embodiment while seeking for spiritual guidance and nourishment, is the possibility of hearing more voices than the normal register we seem to notice.

Each person lives amidst a number of conflicting voices – family, friends, public agendas, commercial pressures, pastoral encounters, entertaining invitations. Often we seek to develop skills to interpret, adjudicate and prioritise wisely in terms of our own response. Modern technology has increased our ability to drown out difficult or strange voices, so as to live in a more conducive 'echo chamber' of our own preferences.

Quiet Attention

Carter highlighted the resources of particular voices to help order what can easily be a cacophony into something which can better fit us for the Kingdom. Often overlooked, and certainly underestimated, is the inner voice of conscience. This still small voice needs the space of a quiet attention: it is significant that Jesus went out early in the morning to be on His own to pray. Prayer is based upon seeking to give space to the light that lightens every person (John 1:1-14) – our capacity to know ourselves to be in the image of God and open to the Holy Spirit – a living word. However, Carter recognised the danger of such a 'voice' being a subtle form of endorsing personal experience. Thus, as we have seen, the voices of the liturgy provided an important context to enable the disciple to recognise and respond to the working of the Spirit in the soul. The voices of the liturgy bring together scriptures, creeds, psalms, sacraments, services for particular occasions.

The Voices of our Neighbours

Then, besides the inner still small voice of conscience as the indwelling Word of God, and the voices of the liturgy to form character and vision, self-awareness and appropriate intercession, confession and the receiving of absolution – Carter also identified the significance of the voice of the Spirit in other people: "love thy neighbour as thyself". If the neighbour is as important as the self, then both voices are vital to inform prayer. This was modelled at Clewer by the sharing in worship of Sisters, associates, clergy and penitents, through a fixed structure of offices. There was a need for prayer to be 'common' as well as personal and private. Besides going out early in the morning to pray alone, Jesus engaged with a huge variety of people by asking them to articulate their 'prayer': "what do you want?" Further, Jesus regularly attended the synagogue and the Temple – structures for what Carter identified as the voice of the church.

In these ways prayer is the key to becoming more fully aware of the self in relation to others and to the shaping of the church. The result will not only enable a richer unfolding of the vocation of a person or particular group, but also it will serve to position such 'calling' within the wider project of the Kingdom coming as light and leaven into society. Prayer needed to be personal, corporate and societal: the danger was to concentrate upon one of these areas and thus undermine the fuller potential of the Kingdom project.

Ordering the Possibilities

For Carter the whole world of the 'rescue' of fallen women too easily became a scheme for personal 'salvation' and redirection, or a charitable enterprise within which individuals could be encouraged to make such a journey, or even a legislative and social programme to improve conditions in society.

The work of the Clewer Initiative flourished because of his insistence in holding each of these possibilities together – in an inter-related dynamic whereby each challenged and reshaped the other. Hence the importance of enabling individuals to find a place in what was essentially a 'religious' order, consecrated for the service of the world.

Listening to a Range of Concerns

The journey would often face the forces of corruption, and could experience periods of apparently being becalmed in the darkness and death of the tomb. The strategy was to be one of having courage to concentrate on what or who might be present at these times of entombment: other anxious disciples, curious bystanders, indifferent passers-by, those who had simply moved on, but also the possibility of knowing the presence of angels.

Further, the very orderliness of a religious community was designed with the intention of providing structures to ensure the consideration of this range of voices, and then give priority to those voices entrusted to the Church – as mediating and measuring forces for assessment and for forward planning. The life of the Spirit was best enabled by the structured ordering of soul and body.

Thus, besides the formal offices and liturgies, there were dedicated spaces for listening, and for hearing the voices together. The Sisters listened to each other in chapter meetings. The penitents used to meet in small groups. Others met to discuss best how to fulfil roles such as trustees or associates. While the liturgy provided a context for the spaces of listening to be joined in a common calling, the discreet areas for prayerful fellowship were a key part of this mix in the ecology Clewer developed.

In each space the same dynamic of humility, confession and mercy were present. Carter emphasised the grounding in being sinners together, in every context, and pointed to St Paul, who orchestrated similar schemes, while owning that he was, nonetheless, "the chief of sinners". Paul made such statements in the present tense. Sin was not a state from which fleshly creatures simply escaped. Rather there was a continuing need for mercy which those leading schemes of care and charity would require for themselves, especially before moving to any kind of judgement of others, such as the penitents. By contrast, for many contemporaries in the nineteenth century there was a strong temptation to locate sin in the apparently more obvious areas of sex slavery and alcohol abuse, and then create a power dynamic of themselves as saviours and the enslaved as sinners. Carter was always clear that the 'leadership' of such 'saving' enterprises – in this case himself and the Sisters for example, should always acknowledge their responsibilities to face up to their own sinfulness – not to better equip them to minister to others (worse sinners?), but more to ensure that the work proceeded on the basis of grace ministering to all involved – helpers and penitents.

A Rule of Life

This perspective helps to explain Carter's emphasis upon confession, spiritual direction, and the value of having a rule of life. The structure of a rule of life was a vital way of ordering the religious journey of each individual, but also of the various groups gathered to play different roles in the overall enterprise. Moreover, a rule of life could never be a final and fixed form of ordering. There needed to be wisdom to adjust and change. An example would be the discussion of the place of vows in the ordering of the community of the Sisters – which occurred over a number of years, with considerable debate and soul searching.[2] Structures are not to provide controls to ensure standards guaranteeing spiritual superiority. Rather, structures were to enable the hearing of voices and the indwelling of the Spirit — amidst all the continuing corruptions faced by soul and body.

Priority to Others

Too easily a structure becomes a resting place from within which the person(s) present make huge assumptions about others. There seems to be an interesting relationship between the distance assumed to be between those in a structure, and others outside, and the degree of confident judgement and condemnation crystallised within that structure and applied to those beyond. Hence the temptation for practising Christians to look down upon prostitutes, for instance. This danger, which constantly surfaced within the ecology of Victorian charity, had to be challenged. Carter had noted the priority that Jesus seemed to give to the voices of the poor and the vulnerable, especially women. He tried to help others involved in the Clewer Initiative to take such voices seriously in a pro-active way. Assumptions fuelled by the ignorance which results from the distance between groups and their respective contexts, needed to be challenged and changed into a presumption that those called to Christian ministry can be the first to say, with St Paul, "I am the chief of sinners", while seeking to pay special attention to the contribution that might be made by voices from the margins.

Spaces for Waiting and Watching

Moreover, in this course of lectures, besides the three days of darkness, and death — the waiting and not knowing — Carter also pointed to the significance of the 'Forty days' in the wilderness. As well as times of concentrated crisis, such as the apparent collapse of hopes and a sense of entombment in darkness and death, there needed to be other, less dramatic but equally significant times for being able to come out of a normal comfort zone to know the testing of waiting in the wilderness. Carter recognised that the term 'forty days' did not mean a literal time span but rather indicated a lengthy time of serious paying attention to voices often drowned out by the pressures of everyday life.

This insight was important in helping to shape the structure of a rule of life for individuals and for communities. Thus he encouraged retreats, and led a large number himself. In our times of almost instant communication and decision making, such structures are often missing – to the detriment of the quality and sustainability of the work we are called to do. Even in the nineteenth century, with the establishment of the railways and a national postal service, the signs of easier communication were emerging. Against such a background Carter was keen to emphasise the vital importance of stillness and waiting – putting aside more personal and immediate concerns – to be receptive to the deeper calling of the Holy Spirit.

Cleansing
Carter coined a challenging phrase. He said that too much of Christian spirituality is about what he called 'surface cleaning'.[3] He was an advocate of what we might call 'deep cleansing'. This requires special resources and effort, and a regular regime. The call to move beyond 'surface cleaning' was a call to every disciple: it presupposed structures and disciplines which would inconvenience the comforts of self and established ways, so that there could be movement and significant engagement with the forces of corruption. The mystery of a gospel framed in death and resurrection is the mystery that despite the human instinct for life, we learn most deeply through loss. The instinct for life encourages accumulation – in material forms as much as in terms of knowledge and good practice. This approach underlies the aspiration in individuals and

organisations for growth and for progress. Such a tendency, Carter recognised, soon becomes another shift towards making a certain set of experiences normative, and a measure for others. A real appreciation of material things, or knowledge, or good practice, depended upon a recognition that any human endeavour only scratches the surface. There is always so much more to touch, to see, to understand, to do. The whole point of the liturgy is to take up the incompleteness of human doing and knowing, and grace them with the mercy that connects and blesses out of that very limitedness.

As a result, structures for shaping the enterprises of discipleship must ever be taken into places of retreat — serious stepping apart from all the voices of the world, the self, the group, even the regularity of church. In the wilderness the surface cleaning that seems to keep our worlds bright and shiny, is exposed as so easily becoming a glossy cover up of the need to face imperfections and corruptions. Through the experiencing of such loss Carter knew that the disciple was miraculously equipped with a faith to continue anew on the way: wiser, more committed, but open to learning and correction, as much as to the more welcome signs of progress and grace.

He led numerous retreats, especially at Cuddesdon at the invitation of Bishop Wilberforce. When he published notes of some of these addresses, he offered a dedication to the Bishop "in grateful recollection of his earnest encouragement on the revival of what has since become an integral portion of the Church's devotional life".[4]

Once again, in his Catholic tradition, Carter knew that scripture, sacraments and creeds, offered by an authorised ministry, were the essential ingredients for deeper cleansing — dealing with corruption and potential well below the surface. The discipline of deeper reflection was a key ingredient of this spirituality.

He pointed to the fact that Jesus meets people in their extreme situations, owning the reality of their limitations, and thus ripe for healing and the greater wholeness of the Holy Spirit. He wanted Christians to learn to own limitation and the power this perspective provided for the energy to pay attention, rather than rest in a place of complacency or hopelessness. The Christian journey is a bold desire to learn and to see more – to receive revelation and new life in the midst of darkness and corruption.

Carter often referred to the powerful biblical image of the desert – a place of emptiness, emphasising loss in a dramatic sense, and isolating individuals or groups in a way which forces recognition of the limitations of their own resources. In the desert normal assumptions are exposed as being in need of something more – for body as well as for soul. The 'more' is the gift of mercy to body, soul and spiritual perspective. The whole Clewer Initiative was focussed upon a particular household – which Carter chose to call a House of Mercy. This structure offered civilisation and wilderness in a potent mix – and became a model for a more contemporary appreciation of the call of the Gospel in a corrupt but grace seeking world.

Fasting
A practical manifestation of this approach was the emphasis which Carter placed on fasting – a way of learning through loss, ie through not receiving, but through seeking a different, deeper form of nourishment. Fasting was a catholic tradition that could cut across lifestyles and viewpoints – calling bodies into a common discipline of denial through which the soul might become more receptive to the indwelling of the Spirit. He felt that the post-Reformation

relaxing of fasting to become an option for individuals, rather than being a discipline of the church, served to encourage 'surface cleaning' and undermined the potential of all disciples to be joined in an obviously earthly way of seeking heaven. Carter recognised, as did the anthropologist Mary Douglas a hundred years later, that fasting could be a more powerful form of teaching and building a common life than any amount of teaching or more tailored schemes of spiritual devotion.[5] Fasting provided a taste of the desert in people's everyday lives, amidst all the understandable efforts to keep any sense of lack at bay. Our instinct for a green and pleasant land needed to be tempered by this too easily ignored element of God's creation. The need to align the management of the body, our physicalness, with the understanding and work of the soul, our spiritual aspiration, was urgent in an age of increasing prosperity for some, and abusive exclusion and oppression for many others.

Fasting was also important to help provide a proper perspective on the role of 'celebration' – thankfulness and joy for our bodies and our physical environment, because better connected to our spiritual aspirations and the blessings of the Holy Spirit. Fasting helps the body know its need of mercy, and enables the soul to focus on the shape and gift of mercy that the Spirit brings to meet us.

For Carter this approach to discipline provided a regular framework for physical awareness, spiritual life, and social connectivity. The rhythm of emptiness and abundance keeps the focus upon the realities of the human condition, and upon the catholicity of the mercy God provides to call fallenness and limitations into being raised up and fulfilled.

Endnotes

[1] T.T. Carter: The Passion and Temptation of Our Lord, Masters 1863.

[2] T.T. Carter: Vows and The Religious State, 1881.

[3] T.T. Carter: The Life of Sacrifice, Masters 1864.

[4] T.T. Carter: Retreats with Notes of Addresses, Masters 1893.

[5] T. Larsen: The Slain God, Oxford 2014.

Clothed in Promises

Covenant

In trying to resource the calling of the Initiative that became the Community of St John Baptist, Clewer, Carter looked to the biblical model of covenant. In a culture of industrial revolution and business expansion, there was a growing concern to develop more stringent understandings of 'contract' — so as best to preserve and secure predicted relationships. Advocacy and enforceability were essential. A similar mind-set can become important for Christian social enterprises, not least because of the need to become competent and trustworthy partners of secular agencies and partners. The Clewer Initiative itself developed models of good 'business' practice in its establishment of premises, laundry work and the appropriate legal framework.

Unequal Partners

However Carter recognised the importance of retaining a notion of the more ancient, biblical notion of covenant. He delivered a sermon about the experience of Noah.[1] The call to take action amidst the darkness and destruction of worldly life, especially the scheme to preserve the animals through providing the necessary structures and organisation. But the blessing and sealing of this initiative was expressed through the gift of a rainbow. A sign of a covenant – God's promise into which future generations of those called to follow in Noah's footsteps were invited to step. And the point that Carter emphasised about a covenant, is that it can signify a relation between two unequal partners, whose mutuality is expressed through commitment, not simply performance. In fact the primacy of commitment is a beautiful sign (the rainbow) which can 'hold' a varying and uneven pattern of actual relationship. For Carter this was the seal of that hope beyond hope – through the 'forty days' of waiting in the wilderness of the vast sea of challenges and corruption – which characterises the Christian contribution to issues such as slavery. A trust in the triumph of life, even through suffering and death. Covenant provided a different kind of risk register to that of a 'contract' approach. Assessments still need to be made, but the 'way' (hodos) may involve detours or visitations that cannot be anticipated. There will always be room for mercy and new life – which will require the wisdom to recognise and respond accordingly. The kingdom project is always God's agenda within which we are called to play particular but always penultimate parts.

Being Clothed in Promise

Carter pointed to the story of Abraham being willing to offer his son, Isaac, his whole 'future' as a sacrifice to the more mysterious purposes of God.[2] Such an attitude of faith in the covenanted promise of God enabled Abraham to notice a different kind of provision that the Lord was making: the lamb caught in a thicket. This was simply a gift from well outside of any carefully 'constructed' script. The key was to give self wholly to the promise of the covenant, and thus to be opened up to the radical power of divine presence, when too easily we are simply concerned by the factors which we had assumed to be our responsibility.

This dynamic of life from the corrupting forces of human limitation, depended upon the ability to pay attention to what God might be offering in a different way. For Carter this reinforced the catholic doctrine of the centrality of the altar for worship in the community, or in the parish. As for Abraham, or Jesus raised upon the cross, the discipline of learning to pay attention to the altar of sacrifice was the key to both receiving the courage to act, well before outcomes could have been safely calculated, and the wisdom to always look wider than what would otherwise be a more immediate or obvious agenda. The altar for Carter was the focus of Christian life bring expressed in its limitations and brokenness, yet graced with the mercy of hope to be embraced in a Holy Communion, a Household of Kingdom energies and securities. Carter called people to become 'a child of this covenant' – a child of the Rainbow promise.

He goes on to say that "God's promise clothes us". As with the experience of Abraham and Noah, despite all the terrors of pressure and destructive forces.

The Clewer Initiative was an exercise in trying to receive this covenant promise seriously.[3] A key indicator was the request which eventually came from the Sisters, to take the traditional monastic vow of poverty, chastity and obedience. Carter explored this agenda cautiously, partly because of the understandable nervousness of Bishop Wilberforce about the enterprise being undermined through accusations of 'popery' in the years when Roman Catholicism was becoming more clearly re-established as part of the ecology of English religiousness.

.

Poverty

Poverty was important as a commitment to the teaching of Jesus: "blessed are the poor". In an emerging market economy, where money was becoming the driver of a materialism that seemed to be the measure of everything, this alternative priority presents an important indicator of the nature of the promise of God – which is to vulnerability and need – not to self-established security and success in worldly terms. The Beatitudes indicate that poverty is both a material and a spiritual condition. For Carter and the Sisters of Clewer, such poverty was important to school them in the integrity needed to be alongside those trapped in involuntary, abusive vulnerabilities, and also to indicate their continuing openness to the riches of the mercy of God as key to their endeavours, rather than the temptation to overvalue the physical structures and measures that need to be a part of every enterprise seeking to serve the ministry of God's goodness and grace. In his teaching Carter made clear to Sisters and penitents alike, that poverty was a vow to put the self at the service of God and His mercy for others. This would provide an important foundation for the style and direction of their work together – and genuine common ground with those who remained vulnerable and in desperate need.

Chastity

Chastity was challenging in a world of double standards about gender and the role of women. Carter argued that chastity involved the recognition that we are all creatures who live by having desires, including sexual desires. To be chaste was to commit these desires to the purposes of God, through stewardship of the body and discipline of the desire: further such a vow included a commitment to contribute positively to the stewardship of other people's bodies and desires. It was never simply a personal discipline – but always a sign. To take a vow of chastity was "self-renunciation, service, habitual obligation".

Such chastity was not simply for members of religious communities, it was for parishioners, and for married as well as single people. The call to live in a chaste relationship with the body, desire and the discipline of these gifts being offered into the world to serve others. Thus, chastity could not be handled simply by a system — it was a spirit, part of God's promise of enabling mercy. Love is to be received in order to be shared — within a spirit of self-control and service to the genuine wellbeing of others — not least in the vulnerabilities of their bodily needs and desires. For Carter chastity therefore constituted a peculiar and sacred alliance with the Spirit of God. He is clear that it is not our choice — it is God's call, emerging and sustained through a "prayerfulness that is honest about our needs, thankful that we do desire to be connected to others, but obedient to God's greater purpose for us and for them". In this way, he described the virginity of these single women called to be Sisters as 'a separated vocation' — not a form of asceticism, rather a call not for withdrawal, but for a particular way of engagement, alongside that of marriage.

Obedience

Finally, with regard to obedience, he was clear that this did not mean uncritical acceptance of particular sets of teaching or patterns of practice. The obedience of Abraham was first to a mysteriously challenging call — not conformity to an established set of guidelines. Obedience is a spiritual state of paying attention and having the courage to set out on the way. Too often the spiritual life becomes a form of negotiation with God and with the self, about refining or changing direction. Carter recognised the danger of personal experience subtly becoming the measure and the guide. Obedience for Christians, and especially for the Sisters taking such a vow, was not about simple conformity, rather it was commitment to be called further along the way of challenge, but always as part of another's agenda.

Vows provided a sharpened focus for the Sisters to promise themselves into God's covenant promise. Such vows were eventually introduced, and played an important part in the formation of a community with an outward dynamic, open to the call of God and the challenges of vulnerability.

Working with Imperfection

In one of his sermons Carter used the image of a worker[4] – some kind of medieval craft person. As an Anglo-Catholic his fascination with cathedrals and church buildings gave him a real appreciation of sculpture, carving and the creation of stained glass windows. A skilled worker learns by working with the materials of creation, and letting the spirit of the Creator create within, in a way that can guide more material outcomes. Each of us is called to be a co-creator: a worker in God's world. Jesus Himself was formed in this way as a carpenter.

A worker 'works': that is contributes to something that connects them with others. They need to learn about appropriate tools and techniques in order to be creative – often by making mistakes or coping with blemishes, imperfections, and by visioning beyond their own capabilities. Carter pointed out that a good worker knows that there are always imperfections. The work could have been done better. Much work is a momentary contribution that wears away: dust to dust. Yet there is something in the work of creativity that speaks beyond any material manifestations, and plays a part in a much greater story. He invited disciples to consider these perspectives, so as to know that there is a call to work, which involves striving for perfection amidst the inevitability of imperfection. When Jesus says "be perfect" it is a call to share in the work of a Father whose essence is the mercy that absorbs and works with imperfection.

The Consistency of Humility

Thus the disciple, including those who formalise their work around vows, should always be conscious of the need for what he called a "consistency of humility" and the way in which our work therefore connects us together through sacrifice, that is through owning and living with imperfection. It is the promise and mercy of God that embraces this humility and sacrifice so that it becomes creative for the coming of the kingdom.

He sometimes referred to the fact that as Israel wanders on a spiritual journey there is a need constantly to stop and build the altar which gives focus to humility and sacrifice in the way of God. Offering imperfection to be blessed with the mercy of God's wholeness or His holiness.

Priestly Ministry

Within this ecology Carter valued the role of a ministerial priesthood.[5] Everyone was called to be part of the priesthood of all believers, but some are called out and prepared to minister the tools and resources God provides for gathering at the altar: in gospel terms these tools were scripture, sacraments and creeds: perspectives and practices to refine humility and sacrifice and to enable a greater receptivity to the grace of mercy. An initiative such as that at Clewer needed to include this contribution of a ministerial priesthood to ensure that the journey of vows/ commitment, service and sacrifice, is always rooted in the life of the Trinity, rather than ensconced in our own shaping and practices.

The priestly ministry of every disciple was called to receive such ministerial priesthood. Too often witness in the world can have a much more tangential relationship to scripture, sacraments and creed. This was another marker for Carter of the nature of mission fed by his Catholic Tradition. Giving priority to these God given resources ensured that the gospel initiative could never be captured or delivered in terms of political promises or programmes: there must always be an openness to wider, less calculable forces, including the primary contributions to be made by the vulnerable and all who recognise the reality of imperfection, for themselves, and for ways of trying to better organise human flourishing.

Infinite Mercy

At the heart of the gospel is the charter that the promise of God tolerates a more challenging degree of imperfection than many well organised people are willing to live with. This is why Judas gives up his discipleship, in exasperation at the palpable gap between ideals and actual outcomes. In a similar tone Peter asks 'so how many times should I forgive – seven?' – only to be challenged with the rejoinder 'not seven, but seventy times seven'. The infinite mercy of God gives a flavour to all our work and initiatives, whether vows for ourselves or schemes in the service of others, which it is always challenging to recognise and receive. Carter called for Christian character to have a depth and elasticity that can cope with the gaps between our aspirations in our work, and the reality of what so often is produced – whether in physical performance, organisation effectiveness, or the clarity of our moral thinking.

Presence and Absence

Carter brought these perceptions together in relation to the story of Jesus meeting the disciples on the road to Emmaus. Jesus can be seen to be exercising a ministerial priesthood, helping them to draw appropriately upon scripture, using the creedal core of faith in God's promise of the hope through the imperfections of suffering, failure and death, and then He shares the sacramental moment of the breaking of bread. Significantly Jesus as ministerial mediator leaves them, to translate these God-given resources into their own everyday lives, and those of their communities. Once on their own, they feel absence and uncertainty, as well as faith and hope. This is the test of Christian living that can benefit from structures such as vows, and commitments to making the altar central to every initiative of witness.

Much discipleship needs to happen on the way, in transit, disconnected from the immediate support of church or formal faith. There needs to be a fundamental realism about being on the road – in the service of Jesus. This was the driver of much Anglo-Catholic social action in the nineteenth century. The sending out of disciples into the appalling vulnerabilities being created by the modernisation processes in the surrounding society. Too often such witness becomes written up as a story of success. It is only when we read the gospel carefully that we notice the absence as well as the presence of Jesus: the pains and pressures amidst the healing and hopefulness.

Gathering towards God

In such testing dynamics Christians needed the support of the community – for character to be formed and held amidst our imperfections as workers and co-creators. The Catholic emphasis upon gathering regularly around the altar, and of moving from nave to sanctuary, from our human gatheredness into God's holiness, needed to be acted out and experienced. Emmaus was an important model for both the nourishment of Christian vocation, and also for accepting the dynamics of a complex and challenging 'way' through the world. The place of mystery, waiting, confessing and praying was crucial – hence his emphasis upon good liturgy – to gather people into a community of mercy, in order to be better equipped to be sent out into the market place of human working.

Carter pointed to the fact that Jesus put a child in the midst of those striving to be His followers.[6] He reminded his hearers that a child is most obviously a picture of a work in progress. Jesus also invited us all to be such children. This helped the penitents have hope and confidence in their future, alongside the Sisters, parishioners and the others who may have felt that their particular works displayed a superior quality. It is in the midst of imperfections that initiatives for the gospel need to be formed and pursued.

Endnotes

[1] T.T. Carter: Mercy For The Fallen: Sermons for The House of Mercy, 1856.

[2] T.T. Carter: The Life of Sacrifice, Masters 1864.

[3] T.T. Carter: Spiritual Instructions: The Religious Life, Masters 1879. 'Studies in The Teaching of The Founder: CSJB Novitiate n.d.'

[4] T.T. Carter: The Spirit of Watchfulness, Longmans 1899.

[5] T.T. Carter: The Doctrine of The Priesthood in The Church of England, Masters 1863.

[6] T.T. Carter: The Imitation of our Lord Jesus Christ, Masters 1860.

10

Caught Up in the Cloud of Prayer

Much of Carter's teaching explored the importance of paying attention – through the liturgy and the tools given to the church such as scripture, sacraments, creeds and the authority of her ministry – to oneself, the context and most especially to the largely unnoticed and unincluded. The key was what he called "the power of prayer."

Promise and Process

Too often the power of prayer can seem to include someone else's prayer: the church, or the spiritual leader, for instance. Carter recognised that each creature, indwelt by the enlightening power of the living Word, was called to recognise a capacity for prayer – for seeking, asking, regretting, giving thanks. Christians give this instinct an intentionality by focusing such reflectivity "through Jesus Christ Our Lord". For Carter this prayer could best be pursued by more consciously seeking to put ourselves into the promise of God, in partnership with His purposes for creation, and in partnership with others called to a similar search for greater goodness and graces amidst the perils and dangers of this life.

In this sense, he understood that prayer was always a placing of oneself more self-consciously into the presence and purposes of God – a process. Too easily prayer became a method or a technique to calm and shape the person praying. By contrast, Carter saw prayer as the paying of attention to the processes and the potentialities of the coming kingdom, in a way which makes those who pray part of the response, as well as part of the reflection that refines and highlights that response.

The Temple Mysteries

With his high church background, he drew especially upon the imagery of the Temple[1] in scripture to explore what this kind of praying might involve, and how it might engage us in the coming of the kingdom. In particular, he examined the teaching in the Book of Exodus, where incense is used in the Temple, between the Altar of Sacrifice and the Mercy Seat of the Divine Redeemer. The Altar of Sacrifice is the place in the Temple to which people come to own their sinfulness and to offer sacrifice. The Mercy Seat is the sign of God's grace and redemption. Between these two important places, twice a day, the priest would go to dress the lamps and burn what the language of the text best translates as "sweet incense". As people come to pray into the promise of God, and in partnership with His purposes and with the prayer of others – all this praying, in its complexity, incoherence, imperfection and hopefulness, is caught up in the sweet incense, which is all pervasive, embracing people, prayers, the Altar of Sacrifice and the Mercy Seat of the Redeemer.

Carter taught that the incense is a sign that if we put ourselves with others on the Altar of Sacrifice, appealing to the Mercy Seat, then the Divine Redemption expands with unlimited grace to embrace us with a reality we can taste, even if it is not clear about the intended or possible effects. Prayer is a form of connection with the promise of God, accepting our part in the Covenant. The task of discerning this renewed sense of hope and direction remains the work of discipleship. Moreover, the sweet incense reminds us that all our prayers are caught up in the process and purposes of God's goodness and grace. Our particular prayers on the Altar of Sacrifice are carried towards and connected with the Mercy Seat of the Redeemer, but always as part of a human response to the call of the kingdom. Prayer, even in private, can never be a purely personal transaction with God – it will always draw us into the public nature of unlimited mercy offered as good news for the salvation of the world.

Too often we approach prayer from a very personal perspective and as a way of seeking greater understanding about our call and its direction as it is unfolding. Both of these elements are crucial to praying, but only as we own our connectedness and common cause with others in a project which is unashamedly political and public – a kingdom. We want to know where we are going when we walk, but in the spirit of Christian prayer, it is only by walking that we find the way. Prayer is seeking direction, but only within a confidence to seek out much that is unknown and needs to be revealed.

Sweet Incense
It is this kind of prayer which was so vital to the entire Clewer Initiative. A paying attention to God's promise, by placing ourselves and our endeavours on the Altar of Sacrifice, always with the humility and hopes of others who are similarly seeking God's goodness and grace. This prayerfulness, for Sisters and penitents, provided a nourishment that gave insight into further possibilities, discipline to pay attention beyond the usual parameters of our

context and world views, and faith to continue to work and act, even into imperfection and the challenges of darkness and corruption.   Carter showed them that such prayer allows everything, seen and unseen, to be caught up in God's desire to give us grace in ourselves, with others and within His Kingdom purposes.   Prayer was placing all of this within the "sweet incense", the presence and pervasiveness of the Holy Spirit felt and tasted, so that the Altar of Sacrifice was not the main focus of our particular concerns, but always an embrace into the presence and power of the Mercy Seat of the Redeemer.

Everyone Included

Carter pointed to one other feature in this important image of the Temple – the Table of Shewbread.   Every Sabbath, twelve loaves were placed on the Table of Shewbread.   The twelve loaves were for the Master and his guests, and since twelve was the complete number of the tribes of Israel, this offering was a sign of total inclusivity. The prayers at the Altar of Sacrifice, caught up in the sweet incense of the promise and redemption of the Mercy Seat, were part of the connecting of all God's people with this process of salvation.   Every person was represented – not just those in the Temple at that moment offering prayers. The Master makes everyone His guest, and part of the process of the kingdom. Therefore, our praying has a representative element too.   Those who pray need to reflect on their relationship to the fullness and completion of God's purposes through the inclusion of every one of His people.   Prayer connects us with a radical inclusivity that will inspire and call us to seek its manifestation in daily life.

Perhaps in our contemporary worship, seeking to be part of a Holy Communion with God and with our neighbours, we should begin the service by placing twelve loaves on a table within sight of our praying. Certainly, the Clewer Initiative learned to pray with this kind of awareness. Prayer was the unique and essential means of placing oneself and one's endeavours in the potential completeness of God's children. It does not depend upon our technique or method or ability to feel holy or blessed, rather prayer is simply seeking to be open to receiving something of God's goodness and grace, for ourselves, with and for others, as part of the all-encompassing glory of the coming of the kingdom. As we walk, embraced by this cloud of sweet incense, the way will become clearer, providing greater courage to face challenges and corruptions and offering richer insight into how to recognise blessing. Carter described such prayer as "the union of the human with the divine."[2] Our small prayers caught up in God's amazing grace.

Such prayer is an attitude to life, pursued through the lens of the Temple and the resources of the Gospel. It brought healing and hope to many penitents who had aspired to certain ideals, but had become distracted and diverted into the darkness of prostitution and abuse. It brought the same grace to the Sisters who made vows to commit themselves to such a practical outworking of "spiritual" practices.

Penitence

Carter, in a Lent course delivered in 1866 with the title "Life of Penitence"[3] suggested a key pointer for a framework for keeping prayerfulness focused in this way. The foundation was penitence, bringing ourselves to the Altar of Sacrifice, because the Prince of Darkness was always pulling us down. The penitent forgoes the instinct to put self at the centre. Rather the foundation is to own our "fallenness", the sin which means missing the targets for which we were made.

The Forgiving Love of Jesus

Next, there must be confident study of the forgiving love of Jesus. In the scriptures, nearly every encounter shows love which forgives, heals, helps, provides confidence and connects with the sweet incense of prayer as a greater power. Forgiving love does not condemn: it gently challenges the penitent to "sin no more" - to pursue their potential to do better. More, Jesus is seen to forgive not just individuals, but groups and communities, a theme Paul picks up with the clarity of his vision to include Gentiles as well as Jews.

Third, our encounter as penitents with the forgiving love of Jesus quickens the power of the Holy Spirit within. It clarifies the desire for wholeness and new light, enabling openness to tasting the embracing sweet incense of mercy. There is a shift from "Lord I am not good enough", to accepting responsibility for playing a part in the kingdom process.

Putting Self Second

Accepting this responsibility of discipleship clarifies the importance of 'putting the self second'. A phrase of breath-taking simplicity and directness. Rather than prayer being a focus on seeking help to get through the day or gain 'solutions' or solace to the great pressures and problems being faced, it becomes a personal commitment to begin from the Altar of Sacrifice – to put the self second.

Cleansing and Renewal

This foundational framework opens up the rich possibilities of Pentecost and Jesus' promise of the Spirit of Truth to lead us into all truth. Baptism is the Catholic sign of being called to live by the discipline of cleansing and renewal that can be regularly expressed through spiritual direction and confession. Not as a means of purifying or developing a particular person in their individual uniqueness, but as a way of ever bringing each disciple to the Altar of Sacrifice, The Mercy Seat of the Redeemer, a place within the completed people of God, all caught up in the Cloud of Prayer.

Truth as Indwelling

This means that 'truth' can never be reduced to a formula or a particular set of practices. Rather what is true emerges in and around the penitent who is not looking for answers, but simply the right sense of direction. The truth of God is held and expressed through the relationships embraced in the Cloud of Prayer. Partial, working expressions of 'truth' will ever be surfaced, to help navigate the darkness and to keep the gaze on the Redeemer. Truth becomes a quality of living in community and working for goodness with others, from this base of relationship. Initiatives like the Clewer project became harbingers of the truth of the Gospel, and were able to contribute to the emergence of more 'truth' in society – both about current situations and with regard to the most appropriate responses. The truth of God is the Redeeming Christ dwelling in His people and guiding their path. This reality was vital to Carter if the initiative to fight sex slavery and other forms of the abuse and the commodification of fellow human beings was to be effective and confident.

Participation in the Promise

The truth becomes an attitude in us which enables confrontation with sin and evil, in ourselves, in others, in the structures and values of society and then, from the Altar of Sacrifice, our prayers out of these imperfect, fallen realities, become caught up in the sweet incense of the Redeemer and His Mercy Seat. We do need to be organised in our thought and reflections, but only as enabling our participation in this greater mystery, rather than such practices reducing the agenda of prayer to a much more personal or immediate focus.

The major challenge is how to bring this prayerfulness into concentrated, institutionalised forms of darkness, such as the smart business practice that has always enabled slavery to flourish. We make a crucial start if, in Carter's terms, we pray to put ourselves into God's promise. Then the sweet incense will be able to touch us with insight, courage and the nourishing of a capacity to both identify and tackle these forces of structural evil. The insight and the energy will be God's, not just ours. Our responses will become consecrated with a divine wisdom, persistence and provocation that will empower the identification of when and how to say 'woe' is this person or practice (woe to you, Pharisees, lawyers, the rich, the satisfied). Such empowerment will similarly provide the grace to associate ourselves with the forces of blessing (for the poor, for the excluded, the suffering, the mourning, those seeking peace and justice). Prayer as explored by Carter points to a spirituality of the Beatitudes (Matthew 5, Luke 6) a scheme of identification and commitment for involvement and societal transformation with the express purposes and values of God's kingdom agenda.

Breathing Our Concerns

And for our encouragement and comfort, Carter recognised that short prayers are enough to keep the incense swirling - when we seem to struggle, he commended "filling up some of the vacant spaces with ejaculatory prayer" – breathing out our concerns and thanks in order to breathe in a far fuller presence and power. Such prayer invites us to participate in something that God is doing anyway. It challenges a long tradition of conscientious Christian anxiety about failing in our spiritual lives and then looking to make more time for prayer, to find richer resources, or more conducive places or postures.

Our Part in Journeying into the Unknown

While these elements are valuable – hence the huge efforts made by the Clewer Initiative to provide carefully designed spaces, tailor made office books and a prayer pattern for devotional practices – nonetheless the key factor was to cultivate an attitude of putting the self second, at the Altar of Sacrifice, in the company of others (seen and unseen) to be caught up in the sweet incense of mercy. This sweet incense is ever swirling in the Temple of God's creation, between the Altar of Sacrifice and the Mercy Seat of the Redeemer. We simply take our part – placing it into this process of prayer, for an unknown journey, where the markers will never be certainties of our understanding or achievements, but simply signs of how the blessings of the kingdom can manifest an ever more inclusive expression of God's goodness and grace.

Endnotes

[1] T.T. Carter: The Spirit of Watchfulness, Longmans 1899.

[2] T.T. Carter: The Value of The Soul – Sermons, Longmans 1875.

[3] T.T. Carter: The Life of Penitence, Masters 1866.

11

A Model of Catholic Mission

Slavery: The Hidden Challenge

Carter found a particular focus for his long Ministry in the parish of Clewer in challenging a brutal form of oppression – highly organised prostitution using the most vulnerable of people. An early echo in our modern world of the commodification of people we now recognise and name as Modern Slavery.

Society needed help both to recognise and to respond to this cruel and abusive business flourishing in the margins of efforts to improve standards and systems for the well-being of all. We face a similar dilemma as the increasingly universal mantra of freedom and rights becomes an idol worshipped by some at the expense of the millions pushed ever deeper into relative poverty, insecurity and inequality. Modern slavery is the most brutal and sharp expression of this confusion around values, practices and any sense of real mutuality.

An Inclusive Response

Carter wrestled with the challenge of how best to respond to the most abused and excluded, in a way that could offer a connectivity between the powerless and the powerful, the strong and the vulnerable. The model of the Kingdom proclaimed as good news by Jesus the Christ was a political form of radical inclusivity: a genuine catholicity of compassion and co-operation within the generous grace of the Mercy of God.

His own calling and formation for Christian Ministry was a journey of learning to recognise that there could be a huge and forbidding distance between organised religion, with its self-preserving structures and values, and the cry in the hearts of those enslaved in oppressive systems of exploitation.

This journey opened his eyes to the temptation to pursue a vocation of making the world fit around himself, whereas the inclusivity of the Kingdom initiative gave priority to challenging and changing the workings of the world in order to better 'fit' and serve those who were most vulnerable and easily unnoticed.

Formation for Christian discipleship in this context involved learning to pay attention more closely to what was happening, and then involving a wide variety of perspectives and aspirations in crafting an appropriate approach to a re-shaping that could bring love, grace and life to despair, fear and isolation.

Call to Reshaping

Christian Faith was owning the call and the courage to act for such reshaping, even if the apparent 'evidence' seemed discouraging or overwhelming. This was especially important in the challenge to discern the prevalence of double standards in regard to gender and in relation to wealth. Without facing these deep-seated cultural and religious attitudes, much work for positive change would be cosmetic and obscuring of the real agenda.

Asset Based Community Development

He began this work in Clewer by recognising the value of resources already present. Instead of the temptation to simply launch a new project, Carter pursued a methodology of what in more recent terms is called Asset Based Community Development. He realised that the church provided structure, resources and patterns of commitment that could be crucial. Thus, while exploring and encountering the full extent of the degrees of enslavement to drink and the sex trade, he gave considerable energy to building up the Body of Christ – the Christian presence and its possibilities and priorities.

This broader understanding of the Gospel and commitment to a wide expression of witness created a clarity of priorities that enabled the more specific Clewer Initiative to be able to find appropriate personnel and support.

The foundation was prayer – the discipline of what his Bishop, Samuel Wilberforce, described as "being upstairs".

Personal prayer and public worship helped people to catch more of the vision and the priorities of the Kingdom Gospel, and this raised up a common spirit of looking at the bigger picture, paying attention to those currently not noticed, and discerning ways of reaching out as agents of a Grace and Love which eagerly sought to minister to those most in need.

Common Ground

This emphasis upon building up the Body of Christ, the work and witness of the church, focussed through prayer and public worship, provided a wisdom and resilience that was to contrast with the more immediate and hasty attempts of some of his contemporaries to design and establish "penitentiaries" – places of rescue and judgement. Charitable work by some, for others. Religion in its more formal and focussed sense, offering 'help' to those outside. By contrast, Carter and his colleagues in Clewer recognised from the outset that 'helpers' and those who presented as needing 'help' were joined together through acknowledging their mutual sinfulness and need for grace. Hence the growing of strategies and structures in which all those concerned were joined in a common endeavour.[1] A 'Catholic' model of mission.

Local Roots

The 'Initiative' began informally, on a very small scale, through local people like Mrs Tennant, reaching out to others in the parish who were commodities in the sex trade. The common ground of place, and of a clear desire for wholeness for individuals, for the community and for society. This first endeavour expressed the key qualities and theological values of the enterprise, but failed because there needed to be a broader base of support, expertise and commitment. Scale was crucial – a balance between creating enough capacity to offer sustained support and fellowship, yet 'small' enough for the strengths of meaningful personal contact and shared local context to play an equally important part.

Broadening the Base

Carter learned to identify a broader range of skills as he involved Harriet Monsell and her clerical brother-in-law, together with partners bringing resources in terms of funding, management and strategic development. Further, he was quick to involve the Bishop as a sign of this initiative being a regular and recognised expression of the Christian gospel. At this stage a 'fresh' expression of church within the setting of the parish.

Religious Ordering

Besides personnel and structures, there was the key issue of language – the term 'Sister of Mercy' proved to be powerful and easily communicated something of the core values and aspirations of the project. Another example was the decision to name the religious order after St John the Baptist – forerunner and pointer towards a fuller engagement with the life and witness of the Lamb of God.

Having begun with the priority of building the Body of Christ, the church, as focus and foundation for mission and ministry in the parish, the establishment of the religious order was a key way of strengthening this fount of service and sacrifice aimed at extending and enriching communion (or community) with others. Thus, there was a key place for prayer, confession, contributing to the functioning of community, and owning the importance of accepting a challengingly wide range of 'vocations' and 'fallings' as all equally precious to the search to be open to grace and share together in mercy. Attitudes shape action, and attitudes need continuing formation and re-formation – for all of God's children.

Father of All

Carter's theological teaching aimed at exposing and clarifying the resources of grace and mercy offered in the Gospel of Jesus Christ, in a way that could make them more accessible and more universal. He stood self-consciously in the Catholic tradition of the Church of England, and he was committed to the priority of the Body, the connected catholicity of the Church, as an essential context for the journey of any individual. The key connector was the Father – an intimate relationship offered to every child in creation. This intimacy was offered as 'mercy' – both in terms of human sinfulness and failings, but also as a grace to heal and engender hope.

Fallen women, victims of sex slavery, were not simply 'rescued' from a nasty environment – rather they were invited to join in the life of an established community, ordered to enable every member to better own their need for mercy, and to better develop their openness to receiving it. All in a common, Catholic, setting and structure.

Inexhaustible Sympathy

The embracing power was what Carter called "the inexhaustible sympathy of Jesus Christ". This sympathy embraced sinners of every kind, including those involved in abuse and exploitation. The call was to step out of the narrow circles constantly created to enable the fulfilment of human lustfulness (selfishness), in order to seek richer forms of identity through being part of a 'Body'. Such a shift led to recognising the structural realities in the wider society which served to encourage and permit these small circles of self-indulgence, which always flourished by ignoring the cost to others. Christ's mercy reaches especially to those most ignored and oppressed by the operation of this kind of structuring in society.

Penitence

A connecting theme in this Catholic commitment to breaking down the abusive realities of self-serving structures was the call to 'penitence'. Carter often taught about this basic condition from which each human being can recognise a need for grace and a deeper desire for richer connection with the true purposes of life.

Thus the discipline of confession was held up as a tested way of every member of a human community being helped towards honesty in owning failures, and reassurance of the breadth and reality of the healing love of the Redeemer.

Another connecting theme dear to Carter was the call to 'mortification', the denial of self in order to make more open space for God's guidance, and so as to offer more to others.

Expanding the Structures

As the Initiative developed, so the internal ordering needed to become more sophisticated, by recognising a greater variety of possible ways of being 'a part' of this enterprise, for example, the creation of space for associates and lay Sisters, and different possibilities for victims who became embraced into the project.

Further, there were extensions to the basic infrastructure: new buildings, a chapel, a laundry. There was a willingness to learn of new possibilities to better face the core challenges, and then to craft appropriate resources. Sometimes mistakes were made, or new approaches tried and then gradually abandoned. But the basic attitude was one of being open to new life and blessing not just in the individuals involved, but in the organisation, the roles for service, and the infrastructure of buildings and equipment.

Eventually this spirit of being open to creating new life was manifested by taking elements of the Initiative to other parishes in England, and then further afield, especially in India and the United States of America.

New Models

These kinds of development highlighted the fact that an Initiative which started as a 'fresh expression' of church to enable a richer response to a particular challenge, soon became a new kind of 'religious ordering'. Thus it needed a momentum and direction of its own. There was an important shift from being a part of the parish, to being a partner. An enterprise with its own structure and approach, contributing to the mission in the parish, but drawn into wider networks of connectivity and partnership.

Mission in this Catholic tradition has the confidence to grow and bless new forms of witness that can be very different, in focus and in style of operation, and yet grounded in the same theology of penitence, confession, communion and community making – aimed particularly at the most vulnerable.

Calling Out

Fundamental to this approach was Carter's insistence upon 'calling out' because there is One who hears. The work of both parish and the Religious order was to help clarify 'the call': and to provide structured opportunities for this way of presenting into the promises of God. Hence the importance of carefully crafted liturgies for particular occasions.

The art of Catholic Mission was to help own needs, recognise grace and accept mercy. The unconditional love of God was ready to be poured into the cries of those who could own and identify their needs – offering themselves into an endeavour to be part of a more whole community. Often this response needed a structure for praying and for paying attention, clearly part of the life of the church and her witness.

Disciplines

Thus differences and dispositions were not to be simply 'tolerated' by a loosely benevolent kindness. Rather identities and issues needed to be owned, and offered through the disciplines of mortification, so that self could be called into communion, in a way which would transform every understanding of identity or vocational direction. Hence his ability to value chastity as a virtue, alongside the state of marriage: both vocations rooted in vows to put the self at the service of others: to practice hospitality and not just seek a comfortable home for the individual.

But these insights, were never simple 'answers'. Carter recognised the reality of needing to live in the present, and aspire to move in particular directions. A Catholic generosity about complexity, the difficulties of journeying to a new state, and the need for patience and forbearance. All steps following God's call into the richer communion of the Kingdom were subject to being tested.

Generosity of Spirit

Generosity of spirit and sensitivity towards others, especially those of different values or perspectives, was the key to preserving the Catholicity of connection, whatever the tensions. The emphasis was to be on pursuing potential and giving others, even those publicly identified as sinners, the space to explore their capacity for a more wholesome engagement with goodness.

Carter's catholicity included a positive and encouraging attitude to those of different perspectives, including worldly debates and ideals. In a letter to Sisters in Calcutta he commented on the value "of interesting books besides your devotional ones".[2] He went on to emphasise "the need and value of your minds being restored and cheered by the many ideas that the modern world of thought and feeling and beauty provides for you. For we have many sides, and one balances and helps the other, and each has its own proper value".

On another occasion he commented, "our plans will naturally partake of an English character, and in some degree at least, of the general tone of modern society. The very principles of Catholicity suggest this. True catholicity is best seen in its power of adaptation to varying circumstance..." Truth should not be confused with knowledge: the markers of the spirit were not signs of intellectual clarity "but the reign of love, beauty, goodness, grace." Not answers, but qualities to be assimilated.[3]

Mercy provided the attitude, the invitation and the forbearance to create this kind of Gospel opportunity. The courage not to judge but to offer love, hope and encouragement. An approach deep in Carter's catholic DNA. He knew, and taught others, that each of us stands before God as a sinner, and the call is to journey together seeking to be 'companions' – together sharing the bread would be the literal meaning of this word.

Evil and Sins Persist

Of course evil and sin were real, and could not be ignored by a naïve optimism. Confession and absolution provided continuing engagement with this reality. The challenge was how to translate an approach easily accessible for individuals and small groups, into a discipline that could help cleanse and renew the structures of society. These 'policy' and 'practice' implications of the Clewer Initiative were explored by Carter and some of his colleagues, including one of his first trustees, Gladstone, through conferences, public teaching, books, articles, and campaigns.

It remains one of the greatest challenges of any Initiatives following in these steps, to be able to identify how best to make such high quality and strategically effective interventions, in the church and in society. Of most pressing concern is the question: how to find modern equivalents for effective intervention in the twenty-first century.

The Limitations of Experience

Perhaps of most significance challenge is his insistence that human 'experience' always needed to be shaped by the tools given to the church for such purposes: scripture, tradition, Reason as access to the mind of God, creeds, sacraments, plus an authorised ministry using these gifts effectively. Too often a scientific, empirical, evidence based society sees these classic Gospel resources as aids to experience, rather than forces to reshape and redefine the values and aspirations we seek to identify.

This goes back to his insistence upon the priority of building up the church to be the defining and refining site of catholicity expressed in a 'holy' communion. The measure is not human achievement, but reception of the Father's connecting love, which comes from the gifts ministered by the church, but also through the voices of others, including the unnoticed and the unlikely.

Paying Attention

Therefore the work of pursuing this kind of Initiative involves careful paying of attention – within the life of the church and to the cries of those suffering from the shortcomings of society. These complexities highlighted the importance of structures for listening, for reflection, for waiting – and a courage to continue to work until fresh light is given.

There is no expectation of perpetual light for our earthly journey in Carter's catholic approach to mission. The reality of darkness, stumbling and failure will always remain part of the mix of the journey, and those involved in Initiatives like the Clewer project must seek resilience and faithfulness.

Sometimes the challenge will be the need for the cleansing of those pursuing such a project, rather than the judgment and call for change in others. Fasting was a way of organising a regular appreciation of this reality.

The Promise of Mercy

The comfort of the Gospel was always the promise of God's mercy – the new covenant. He held that the classic way of placing the self into such a promise – the vows of poverty, chastity and obedience, still had great value in the modern world. Not for all, but certainly for those keen to commit themselves to a particular calling within the ecology of the overall project.

The more general principle was a willingness to work with imperfection, while seeking appropriate means always to receive the gift of greater perfection through the mercy of God.

Worship and Formation

Public worship provided, for Carter, a very clear way of entering into this promise, and being able to taste the 'incense' of God's mercy without having to subscribe to a particular kind of experience or theological explanation. There was a 'catholicity' of generous connectivity which could be known or understood in a whole variety of ways – yet always focussed upon what he identified as the Altar of Sacrifice (owning imperfection and sin). This was the desire to look towards the Mercy Seat of God's grace, and the sweet incense that embraced every prayer into both of these realities.

The catholic 'completion' of this scene was provided by the presence of the twelve loaves on the Table of Shewbread: a sign of the inclusion of all God's children equally embraced in this spiritual dynamic of cleansing and renewal.

Here was a picture of encounter, together, with the forgiving love of Jesus, the call to put self second, and thus being called into a place to receive the cleansing which enables participation more fully in the promise of the salvation of the world.

Enabling Initiative

The Clewer Initiative emerged from a priest in a parish paying attention to the needs of God's children, and challenged by the organised, systematic, abusive exploitation of a whole host of people not easily noticed within the normal workings of society. A flexibility to work with those who associated, learn from mistakes, value the subtleties of scale and the importance of structuring quality, enabled the foundation of a project which flourished in making an effective response to what we might call Modern Slavery.

Further, these qualities provided an enduring momentum for continuing creative development, first within the parish, then alongside the parish, and finally in other very different contexts. Existing assets were mobilised, developed and shared more widely.

The same process can be discerned in the development of the teaching and wisdom of T.T. Carter – both to nourish the Initiative and its adherents, and also to provide a theological framing for a catholic approach to mission. This was based upon relating to the particular context, and especially the cry of the most needy within it, rather than a more generalised gospel aimed at everybody.

This refinement of focus, a priority for the poor, paradoxically provided the foundation for a proper catholicity. A movement of radical inclusivity in sharing the cries of the heart, the gifts God provides for refining and responding to those cries, and the promise of wholeness which is the Father's will for the whole world.

Continuing Initiative

The challenge for the continuing Clewer Initiative is how best to marry these practical and these theological expressions of catholicity, so as to be better equipped to serve the victims of Modern Slavery, to challenge and involve creatively, both the perpetrators, and those who assent and therefore tacitly allow this crime through simple indifference. There is a need to articulate a wisdom that can feed and shape all those involved: and offer an attractive invitation to partners and other elements of society to play their appropriate part. All these responses are elements of a catholic model of mission, and essential to the continuing contribution of an Initiative formed through the collecting vision of a House of Mercy – for ourselves, for others, for the blessing of all God's world. The sign and measure will continue to be the cry of the enslaved, and the response of the Body of Christ.

Endnotes

[1] T.T. Carter: Parish Teachings: The Apostles Creed and Sacraments, Masters 1882.

[2] The Founders of Clewer, Mowbray 1952.

[3] T.T. Carter: The Spirit of Truth – Sermons, Longmans 1875.

12

The Clewer Initiative Today

The current Clewer Initiative was established in the autumn of 2016, and launched formally on 17 October 2017, at Lambeth Palace. Beginning as a national initiative, sponsored by the Sisters of the Community of St John Baptist and the Church of England. Yet this Initiative, like its illustrious predecessor, first grew in much more local soil, the Diocese of Derby. This dynamic between local earthing and the support and oversight of the National Church is an important factor: both elements have a key part to play.

A Global Concern

The formation of the model for responding to the evils of Modern Slavery was driven by practical engagement with the needs of victims, and the development of partnerships with other agencies. A wider frame came from the declaration to combat Modern Slavery signed by the Pope, the Archbishop of Canterbury and a large number of faith leaders on December 2nd 2014 in Rome.

Further on 7th February 2017 the Archbishop of Canterbury and the Ecumenical Patriarch hosted an international conference on Modern Slavery in Istanbul, which produced a joint declaration promising further work together.

A Local Response

More locally, for those of us in the United Kingdom, the key is to discern how churches can contribute appropriately, alongside the responsibilities and resources of others.

The Role of the Church

There are a number of important areas. First, churches often have a convening power. People generally credit churches with being on the side of goodness and grace, but with no detailed agenda or strategy, as might be the case with statutory agencies or NGO's. The latter groups have public agendas, budgets and targets. Churches can invite these elements into a space for mutual engagement, sharing and collaboration. Yet the connector is good will and an unshakeable faith in the future and the power of goodness. The calling of the Church is to proclaim and enable this life-giving and encouraging perspective. In the Gospels, this power is named as Love: The Love of God, expressed through love of neighbour.

Partnerships

Second, churches are often in networks through which they can bring voluntary energy and commitment into the mix. At a time when statutory bodies face huge pressure on budgets and their deployment of resources, the provision of premises for victims, or personnel to be present for interviews, or care when formal time periods expire, can be hugely significant. Besides a properly professional contribution to these kinds of activities, Christians bring the faith which willingly goes the extra mile for the sake of those in need, and at a cost to themselves.

Next, churches bring skills in partnership working across the complexities of contemporary society. Parishes, Dioceses, the National Church, contribute to models of good practice, such as lunch clubs or pastoral visiting schemes, as well as the ability to reflect upon these practical acts of service in terms of their implications for policy and priorities in the ordering of wider society. There is an important contribution to be made from the perspective of real grass roots engagement informing the questions and the signs of good practice, that need to be put to Government, Local Authorities, the Police and other potential partners. Because the Church shares the experience of the vulnerable alongside its contribution towards the role of professional expertise in social systems and policy, the offer can be a significant factor towards improving the breadth and the effectiveness of possible response, rather than allowing a more limited focus upon simply seeking a set of 'answers' demanding implementation.

Asset Based Community Development

The Clewer Initiative is seeking to explore what might be learned and more widely shared from these kinds of perspectives. The approach is based upon the notion of Asset Based Community Development. There is a presupposition that many of the resources needed for this project against Modern Slavery are already present as potential assets in local communities and in established agencies. Such assets need clearer identification and then development, both in their local context and within the wider wisdom and practices of national and regional demands and pathways for effective actions. This has certainly been the experience in the Diocese of Derby. Existing 'assets' of people, experience, connections and skills, both within the Church and among partners, have been identified and brought into a strategic frame which enables a more effective response to the challenges of Modern Slavery. The identification and consolidation of such assets and the new insights and energies released, have highlighted Carter's wisdom about paying attention to those God sends and giving serious time to a prayerful reflection that can begin to reveal new synergies and possibilities.

Using the methodology of Asset Based Community Development, the convening possibilities of the Churches, the provision of voluntary energy and commitment, and the momentum that can be generated by partnership working, the Clewer Initiative operates by inviting Dioceses and local churches to consider their own current and potential involvements – as an approach to an appropriate witness to the Gospel of Jesus Christ in an age dominated by the forces of commodification – including the brutal commodification of people: sisters and brothers.

Flexible Operating

In order to better co-operate with the Police, Local Authorities and other key partners, such as Safeguarding Officers, there is a need to be flexible about geography. Just as the original Clewer Initiative moved out from one parish to other parts of the country and then abroad, so there is a need to be willing to work regionally and in other structures beyond the parochial or the Diocesan.

Similarly, there is inevitably an international dimension to a Slave Trade that knows no borders, and seems to specialise in destabilising and manipulating people by bringing them into a 'foreign' environment. An important role of the Initiative is to enable more local involvement to be informed by, and contribute to, the challenges of this international dimension. In this area, the Anglican Communion and the Roman Catholic Church provide especially valuable networks.

Gospel Signs

In all of these aspects of the Initiative there will be an important element of the Christian contribution being better shaped to be leaven and salt within the mix of a broader effort involving many other agencies and operators. Yet such an approach will always be consistent with, and informed by, the Church's own contributions in particular contexts – signs and moments offered into the lives of victims and communities – who always need space to be able to discern and craft their own recognition of blessing and its implications in their daily lives. The Clewer Initiative was always a contribution that respected the integrity and preciousness of victims, partners and particular programmes. The Founders never set out to establish a religious order – the detailed structuring of their response emerged as they grappled with the primary issues of the manifestation of evil and the call to witness to the possibilities of goodness and grace. There needed to be space for new life to emerge.

Targets for Today

The new Clewer Initiative, supported by the Community of St. John Baptist, has been established around a number of targets. The methodology of Asset Based Community Development is being used to enable Dioceses and Church Networks to develop strategies, with appropriate partners, to detect instances of Modern Slavery in local communities and to co-operate around the provision of victim support and care. Areas of intelligence raising and pastoral resourcing are especially important in this work.

The Initiative aims to contribute to the building of capacity for detection, support, prevention and the development of good practice. The emphasis is upon deploying existing assets and recognised responsibilities in a collaborative manner, to avoid duplication or competing for resources and roles. In this way assistance to Dioceses and networks seeks to be carefully tailored to specific contexts and needs. There is no 'Clewer Initiative' agenda to be imposed, rather a desire to model the power of partnership where there is adequate potential and energy – not least by celebrating and working with existing enterprises. Attitude is the key to right actions.

A Model for Mission

The project provides a model for the Church's mission in our contemporary context – both in terms of giving priority and effective support to the most vulnerable and marginalised groups and individuals, and also as a sign of how the Gospel can make an effective witness which has credibility and embraces a whole range of partners. God's grace identified in all kinds of people, and accepted as the driver of the kind of generous service of others that transforms darkness into light.

Historically the original Clewer Initiative was based upon clearly demarcated communities, the parish and a religious order. The modern successor recognises the importance of 'belonging' to communities, yet acknowledges that many people remain on the edge, or beyond the fringe of formal arrangements. This poses one of the most interesting challenges to contemporary approaches to mission. An approach which perhaps has more resonance with the New Testament account of encounter bringing healing and hope, yet often not moving to any more formal 'connection' with the organisation or specially structured ways of enabling the practice of faith. Our presuppositions about 'belonging' are being challenged by the dissolution of many of the traditional structures for family, community, church or established organisations.

As the church searches for more flexible ways of offering engagement with the Gospel and tasting the grace of God's loving mercy, the projects being pursued by the Clewer Initiative could have a great deal to contribute – both in terms of practical ways of working and in terms of a missionary theology, which can be confident in the offering of God's grace as seeds of mercy which will flower in ways not necessarily captured by the institutional church.

Growing Resources

Mapping current activities and producing resources will provide tools which can be useful at all levels of this operation. This approach enables the identification and sharing of good practice, the organisation of networks for learning and support, and the analysis of possibilities and problems to better inform future planning and performance within the partnership approach.

There is a particular emphasis upon the provision of effective training opportunities and the gathering of reflective feedback. A website has been established www.theclewerinitiative.org as a forum for these endeavours. The Clewer Team also offer assistance with building local ownership of possible resources, framing a strategy and operational plan, mentoring for key personnel and regular means of evaluation.

The aim is to better enable awareness raising, intelligence gathering, victim care and support and appropriate contributions to local partnerships. There is also scope for churches and networks to engage within their particular contexts with the need to help businesses become more aware of the importance of developing good practise in supply chains. Similarly, in many areas existing work with prostitution and the sex trade can be linked to this wider perspective about Modern Slavery.

Unlocking the Potential

The key premise is that many of the resources needed to tackle modern slavery exist within local communities — but they need to be unlocked, mobilised and leveraged in a strategic way, especially through the operation of effective partnership. The Gospel trusts in potential often before measurable signs of it are discernible for human assessment. This call to walk by 'faith' in the way of new life is of essential significance in a context dominated by a crude sense of utilitarianism.

A National Initiative

Further, the development of a national network through the Clewer Initiative aims to offer a clear sense of direction to the whole Church, and ensure responsible linking with areas such as safeguarding and work with vulnerable children and adults, besides trying to provide strategic alignment with the lead being taken through the Council of the Chief Constables of Police Forces. Further there is provision to enable the Church to develop training and resource materials that can contribute to the urgent need for effective response at a number of levels — local, regional and national.

A Way Ahead

When Carter began his work in Clewer he had nothing like a five year plan! His spiritual discipline and Catholic vision committed him to paying attention to the needs of his society, through the double lens of local reality and the cries of the unnoticed and excluded. The amazing development of the Clewer Initiative depended upon local resources, creative partnerships and a deep listening to those whose lives needed not just protection, but permission and possibilities to aim higher — for themselves, and as contributing members of a society challenged to seek and practice goodness for all.

This dynamic between grass roots engagement shaped by the potential of so called 'victims', and the development of structures and policies for parishes, churches, government, statutory and other voluntary agencies, provides the core commission of the Clewer Initiative. Carter was clear that such work required both helpers and 'victims' to be joined in a common recognition of limitation and proneness to sin (missing the mark). Thus the importance of deep reflection in the context of public worship and personal spiritual direction. The gifts of scripture, sacraments and creed, offered through an authorised ministerial priesthood, were essential elements to be available to all who supported and became engaged in the work. Many were more concerned about the practicalities of doing good work in a charitable spirit. There will be a similar challenge to our own responses. How to root a Gospel project in the proper catholicity of the Church, giving generous freedom for a variety of views, values and offerings, while maintaining an integrity to the Church's participation that is informed, shaped and sometimes re-shaped by the cleansing, forgiving, inexhaustible love of God in Jesus Christ.

Slavery and Salvation

These insights and priorities from the original Clewer Initiative provide an important framework for the outworking of a contemporary response to the evils of Modern Slavery. They raise important questions for the practice of the Church in this area of contemporary life, and for how best such a concentrated 'gospel' approach can be leavened into partnerships which, understandably, are stressed with more immediate concerns about performance, viability and smart development.

Yet this kind of Initiative offers two related opportunities. First, it provides an absolute, public litmus test to enable a positive answer to the frequently posed question of whether or not the Gospel of Jesus Christ has any relevance to the modern world. Second, such an Initiative is poised to play a creative part in the crafting of a viable response to the disintegration of social cohesions, the marginalisation of religion as a public factor, and the widening divide between those who are learning to survive in a globalised marketplace, and those who are simply being excluded and exploited.

On both of these fronts the values, methods and universal sense of responsibility which lie at the heart of the Gospel can offer vital resources both to the urgent fight against this ever increasing brutalisation we call Modern Slavery, and also to the desperate need for models and rationales for better citizenship. Two sides of the coinage which provides the currency of citizenship for the Kingdom of God.

The Clewer Initiative seeks to offer a very small contribution to both of these huge contemporary challenges. Always in humble partnership with others, open to new learning and new ways, but firmly rooted in the Catholic claims of the Gospel of Jesus Christ – the model and miracle of living, suffering, dying and being raised from the dead.

A Gospel Initiative

This was Thomas Thellusson Carter's conviction. One shared by the Community of St John Baptist, Clewer – and a conviction central to the aspirations of the churches to discern and develop a response appropriate to our own context.

The enduring challenge, which Carter and all those associated with him consistently recognised, remains that encapsulated so succinctly in the Lord's statement "You are the salt of the earth;

but if salt has lost its taste, how can its saltiness be restored? It is no longer good for anything, but is thrown out and trampled underfoot". (Matthew 5[13] NRSV).

A challenge and an opportunity for a Gospel Initiative.